The Healing Circle

Monika Arenth

ISBN: 1491069902
ISBN 13: 9781491069905

I want to dedicate this story to my husband, the love of my life and to my fellow nurses who have supported me and one another throughout our journey of healing.

Ein Traum ist unser Leben

Ein Traum ist unser Leben
auf Erden hier.
Wie Schatten auf den Wolken schweben
und schwinden wir.
Und messen unsere traegen Schritte
nach Raum und Zeit;
und sind und wissen nicht in Mitte
der Ewigkeit.
         Johann Gottfried von Herder
A dream is our life
A dream, a dream is our Life
on earth here.
Like shadows on clouds we are
floating and fading.
And measure our idle steps
according to space and time;
and are not knowing in the midst
of eternity.

Chapter 1

Intrusions

Time: 1960

Place: A small medieval town in the heart of Germany

In the beginning there was a bed and under that bed was a girl hidden among the dust bunnies hiding rows of dilapidated slippers. It was a hospital bed, quite high off the ground providing a fairly good hiding place for a small person. She laid flat on her stomach, not caring about the dust and the way she was smudging her best summer dress, the yellow one with angel wing sleeves and fancy flower embroidering on the front. Anytime she heard someone entering the room, by the creaking of floorboards and the door, she pressed her cheek to the linoleum. After holding her breath for as long as she could, she took in big gulps of disinfected air, burning her nose and throat like acid. She could smell it on her hair for days until it was washed again, even though it was brushed into two tightly braided pigtails clamped shut at the bottom with brown plastic clips with yellow flowers.

She did not mind the dust and the dirt and the assaulting smells, for she had to be there, hidden away. Children were not allowed in the hospital ward and this was the only way she could be near her grandmother, who was recovering from stomach ulcers. She would sneak into the hospital, crawl around the concierge's desk and peek down the long corridor to make sure that the coast was clear. Hiding behind a large linen cart, she waited until the door to Granny's room opened. Scanning the room quickly for any doctors and nurses, she would fly in, hug Granny briefly and roll under the bed.

The ward had six beds, all occupied by various grey-haired ladies. They were all accomplices in the crime, for they never gave her away. From her vantage point she observed the ongoing pulse of healing. The coming and going of soft rubber soles, the screeching wheels of the medication and dinner carts and the dusty breeze when sheets were changed and blankets fluffed. She did not even mind the odors assaulting her tender nose, nor the cries and moans of the patients when they were being handled. It was all too fascinating!

Six different diseases gathered all in one room; six different people, personalities, voices, smells. She loved medication time. Some of the elixirs being spooned out smelled pungent and alcoholic, the teas were either sour or sweet and the steamy odor reminded her of the many different plants and grasses she would rub between her fingers when she was walking through a field. It was a strange habit she had and one that Granny disapproved of; grasping leaves and blossoms from shrubs and rubbing them between her fingers until they disappeared. She found the lingering aroma of those plants quite spicy and intoxicating. Often she would pick a great bouquet of all different kinds of wild flowers and twigs. Granny would help getting them cut to fit into vases and always explained the names and purposes of each leaf and blossom.

"This is chamomile, looks like a little daisy, but smell! When you crush its yellow head, hmmm, just like the salve we put on sores and cuts, ha, and this is a mint twig, see the hairy leaves, the blue blossom, smells like chewing gum, doesn't it? This here is catnip, looks like mint, but much more potent. We can steep its leaves in boiling water for a calming drink and watch the neighborhood cats join in for the party, they think we are having!" Grandma's doctor and apothecary were her garden and the neighboring fields. She knew what and when to pick and how to preserve it. It was an art the girl admired and was eager to learn.

Now she was worried, with Granny being so sick and in the hospital, would they know the right leaves and blossoms to prepare to make her better? She looked with suspicion at the white, red and blue pills and capsules Granny had to swallow in great quantities, or so it seemed.

When the door closed and all the nurses had left, she would crawl out of her hiding place to cuddle up next to Granny on the bed. After the patients were given their dinner trays and left to their own devices, she was brave enough to peek under the covered plates. How in the world was poor Gran to eat this, she wondered silently. It all looked like vomit and smelled worse. Granny, reading her thoughts, said:

"I have a sick stomach; everything is boiled without spices and butter, so it will be bland and not aggravate the ulcers."

She did not believe her and thought this could only make her worse or even kill her. Gran picked up the spoon and tipped it into the mess:

"Come, try a little, it's not so bad!"

"No way!" She clamped her mouth shut, gagging just at the thought of having to swallow a bite.

Just before all the women had finished their meals, she hugged Granny quickly and said her good-byes. She slipped out again unnoticed, back out into the hallway, behind the linen cart and down the stairwell. Mission accomplished!

She ran home as fast as she could, down the street, away from that dreadful place with the awful smells and the air so thick with fear!

At home nobody missed her, for she told everybody that she was spending time with her schoolmate across town. Everyone was too busy to notice her wearing her yellow dress; the one Granny had sewn for her. Well, it was just par for the course, children were not allowed to be heard and only occasionally to be seen, preferably clean with sparkling faces and scrubbed hands and nails with their half-moons perfectly shaped and definitely without black smudges. Unfortunately her hands never passed inspection. She had diagnosed her permanently stained fingers, dirty nails and ragged nail beds as an affliction, she had to endure. She considered it a malformation of the fingernail. In her case the fleshy part of the finger was too far removed and left a gap, where dust and dirt could settle. No matter how often and how short she cut them, there was always a grey smudge. She developed the habit of hiding her hands, either balling them into fists or merely sitting on them when she felt observed. In an effort to keep her nails clean, she decided to chew them and her cuticles, which unfortunately achieved the opposite effect.

It was a vicious cycle! A curse! There was only one day a week when her hands and her whole body felt spotlessly clean and soft. It was the day of the Saturday bath, when she could soak in a tub of hot soapy water as long as the water stayed hot.

In the hospital room she gave no thought to possible contamination. There had to be colonies of germs; bacteria and viruses living happily within their dusty confines under Granny's bed no matter how much disinfectant was being used. She did not know about them, so they did not exist. The people's constitutions were strong and their environment mostly unspoiled. They were not afraid of infection, it was not expected, so it did not happen.

From her vantage point under Granny's bed she was able to observe the effort of healing in that hospital setting. The shoes the nurses were wearing were generally white and their soft crepe soles made little sound, while the doctor's black polished leather loafers came with an assertive click. Best to stay out of the way of those shiny apparitions, marching like soldiers from bed to bed, ready for battle with disease and pain. The softer shoes had mostly grey stockined sturdy legs in them, most often shy of ankles. Those black seamed grey clad calves curiously tapered into the solidly tight shoes. If the shoe was black and the calf grey it belonged to a special breed of healer, the Diakonissen Nurse, an order of protestant nuns ordained to become nurses. If the shoes were white, or sandals or even a wooden clog and the ankle and legs appeared slimmer and shapely, they almost always belonged to either student nurses or nurse's aides laboring under the rigid eye of the Diakonissen ward sisters in charge. 'Woe is me,' she thought, 'if any of them would ever discover me in my hiding place.'

When it was really busy, it was not unusual for her to share her spot with a freshly used bed pan. She was always surprised that urine could come in so many shades of yellow, from the palest light green to bright yellow and deepest ocher color. The odor varied just as much as the color, sometimes lemony clear with a hint of ammonia to the threateningly strong with an ill stench, that nearly sent her fleeing her hiding place. Because the hospital ward was run with military efficiency by those eagle eyed nuns, it was never too long until all used containers were cleaned to sparkle and put away properly.

When Gran was resting, she would listen to the conversations of the other five women patients in her room. There were many things she did not understand, jokes about their husbands and children. They were simple small town and country folk; some had strange dialects and their often sexually loaded insinuations left her wondering. She got to experience the great camaraderie among those six who helped one another and only rang for the nurses for tasks they could not do for each other. For instance, the ones who were able to get up fetched things for those on bed rest. The steady ones helped the weak, the recovered lifted food trays and water glasses. What a concept: the stronger helping the weak and disabled! She thought it was a great sisterhood, sharing jokes and often tears. The younger nurses and the ones not overburdened by responsibility and self-importance shared in the fun. That's why Granny never wanted to be in a private patient room.

"What nonsense," she would counter, when her fancy son wanted to pay for a single room for her.

"Be all by myself, forgotten somewhere down the long corridor, absolutely not, we have a community here, we help each other to get better. The ones that are too sick to join in the fun are by themselves soon enough!"

Single rooms were generally feared, for they meant that there was no hope for the sick, for they were dying alone somewhere, as not to depress the others. After hearing those words the girl was on a new mission. She wanted to get into a dying room, to observe somebody really sick, not those joking and carrying on semi-sickies, but the experience of the real thing, the dying! Her wish was granted the following week.

Just as she was sneaking into the room at the usual time, she observed a pair important looking loafers with a snappy heel patting into the room. Those long black shiny shoes, adorned with black socked ankles and wide swooshing black pants, could only mean that a doctor had entered the sickroom. He seemed to be going from bed to bed, standing at the foot of each assessing the charts which were hanging on a hook at the foot end of the bed, bearing the name, disease and temperature curve of each victim. Since he was the doctor, he did not have to speak to the people directly, but questioned mostly the accompanying ward sister, who hobbled diffidently behind him on broad white rubber soles. When he approached Granny's bed, the girl made herself as thin as possible, as to stay exactly in the center of her hiding place. The doctor asked sister, she answered, and then he spoke back to her, which she in turn interpreted into simpler language that the patient was able to understand. For instance he would mumble:

"The tachycardia seems to be subsiding; we can cut down on the antiarrhythmic!"

While the little old wrinkled lady was gazing expectantly at the man's face, hoping for good news or at least for a benevolent smile, the ward sister would explain:

"You are doing much better; your heart is getting stronger, so we can give you less medicine."

And so it went, stalking from bedside to bedside until all six were addressed in that fashion. Then the big black shoes, followed by the thick soled white ones being propelled by heavy blue veined legs, exited the room.

The girl had kept quiet and was carefully listening to this strange new language. She thought it exciting. She had heard different tongues before, but this seemed to be a whole different species. To her it was a secret code which held life and death in its balance. Although she was much too young to understand the significance of any of this, she felt intrinsically a desire to learn more; some might refer to it as a calling! Perhaps at this stage it was only a curiosity born out of boredom and loneliness. She had a habit of devouring books by the dozen and after exhausting the children and youth sections from the library sneaked all the adult books with her Gran's library card. Most adults were just so excruciating slow and boring. It was excitement she craved!

Today she said her goodbyes earlier and hid out in the hallway behind the linen cart, just long enough to be able to scan the layout of corridor. When the coast was clear, she ran to the end of the hall, where she had previously seen nurses go in and out with various implements. Hidden in the doorway of the adjacent room, she peaked into the open door. Lo and behold, it was the single room, she had heard about. The door was partially open, when she snuck in. At first she thought the bed was empty, for all she could see were many pillows and blankets. Upon closer inspection she recognized a human form placed on its side, one pillow under the head, one between the legs and one pushed into the body's backside to keep it from toppling back and lots of covers on top. One blue veined bony hand rested on the blanket attached to an arm so thin that it was really only an arm bone strung equally with blue veins under transparent skin. The almost hairless head was perched high on the pillow. A large bulbous nose pushed a fleeting chin into its folded neck. There were no lips but a gaping hole, shaping the blueish mouth into the letter O. Air was rushing in and out, making the body struggle with each breath. The only motion being the puffing of air while a thin thread of yellow spittle billowed from the side of the mouth collecting on the strategically placed folded towel. The rest of the whole curious figuration was as pale as the bleached sheets it was placed upon. There were no tubes or bags attached to the body. Nothing but air was going in and coming out. This person, man or woman, it was impossible to tell, was clearly spending his or her last days in this single room attended by the sisters only. She doubted the important black loafers would have entered there, for there was nothing to translate, since this poor form did not appear to be awake, even though the eyes were open, staring unseeingly straight ahead into the grey green painted wall.

She thought it fascinating and frightening at the same time. Walking all around the bed, she noticed clean linen other than the spittle, yet there was a definite odor, one even the carbolic acid could not eradicate. It was different from the human smells of the ward she had grown accustomed to. This smell was confusingly pungent and sweet at the same time, that it made her gag. Fighting the urge to leave she ducked around the bed to catch the gaze of the person at eye level. There seemed to be no response so she stuck out her fingers and touched the bony hand lying on the blanket. It felt icy cold and damp. She quickly pulled hers back, as if shocked by static electricity and wiped the dampness on the folds of her skirt. Looking carefully at the icy hand she discovered tiny beads of sweat clinging to the pale skin.

'This body is breathing hard and sweating!' she thought, 'How interesting.'

She could not ponder this any further, because she heard voices in the hall outside the door.

Quickly she made her escape down the back staircase into the main hall of the hospital. She ran past the surprised receptionist through the double doors glad to be outside from this awful sight and smell. Outside she took big gulping breaths of cool fresh air and sunshine. She would not stop running until she was almost home. Breathing hard and sweating through her underclothes, she arrived with a pounding heart and disturbing thoughts buzzing around in her head that made it difficult to act normal around her family.

Several sleepless nights and torturous dreams followed this experience. She always woke with her heart pounding, having the sweet odor of decay in her nostrils and feeling the sticky sweat on her palm, knowing with absolute certainty that this poor creature, she had intruded upon was not anymore among the living. He or she was released from this drab single room, staring with non-seeing eyes against a grey green painted wall. Her only regret being that in her haste and overwhelming curiosity she did not have the grace for a comforting word.

Just to be sure and to make up for her failings, she did return the following day to check on the abandoned soul lying in the single room at the end of the corridor. She had felt no life in the damp hand and had witnessed the struggle, so it came as no surprise to her to find the room deserted. The door stood open, fresh air was flowing through the wide open window, the bed was stripped and the mattress was standing on its side to air. In spite of the breeze the room had not lost its penetrant odor of decay, its sweetness still obvious. Looking outside the window, catching her breath, she felt peace and pondered this fact of life:

'It's a struggle to be born and a similar fight to depart. One can only hope the ride in-between is worth the fuss.'

A wren appeared on the branch of the birch-tree near the window, tilting its little head to one side and greeted her with his song. Then a much harsher sound pulled her back from her reverie:

"Angelika, you sneaky little devil, you have been found out!"

Chapter 2

Granny

In spite of the horrible food, Granny made a full recovery and was released a few days later. Angelika was much relieved, for those daily trips to that dreadful hospital had taken its toll. She had nightmares and was very tired and distracted during school hours.

"Angelika, where in the world are you? Focus!" It was a constant reprimand from various teachers. But then it was difficult to concentrate on math and verbs when one had to sort out sickness and death, which is never far removed when one is brought up by old people. Even older ones come and visit and when they stop visiting, more often than not they are no more.

Abandoned by her parents as a baby, she had never known another mother but Granny and did not miss any. Besides Grandmother there was a grandfather, uncles and aunts and a slew of cousins to make life more interesting. It was Grandmother she adored, for she was a healer in every sense of the word. Much later, a mother herself, she wrote this little prose poem about her. It describes her perfectly!

Grandmother is tall

Grandmother is tall. She is 5 foot 3, reaching almost all the way up
to the kitchen ceiling. I know, because when I stood next to her, I had to bend my neck back to see her eyes.
She was tall and beautiful. Her skin was soft and smooth and had
the color of freshly sliced brown bread.
Someone said her face was wrinkled. I thought, wrinkled is good,
I hope to be wrinkled someday soon.
Her hands were hard and dry, cooling my forehead when I was sick in bed.

Her palms showed signs of hard work and water.
Creams and salves belonged to the weak and incapacitated souls;
she pitied, prayed for and healed. She did not salve her hands in
between tasks.
Her movements were quick and sure and she made you feel yours
could be too.
Her hands were healing hands, as if her strength
could seep into your body. I am sure it did, for I always got
better.
Her eyes were hard to see when she stood straight, for she was
tall.
When she bent down to touch you or tie your shoelace, they
were golden brown with gold specks or were they green?
Her arms were soft with loose flesh, much different from my
own brown stringy limbs.
She smelled of spice and her embrace was that of a cloud,
soft and warm.
I loved to hear her voice; she sang and prayed with an astonishing
energy inside and out. Her singing voice reverberated throughout
house and garden when she went about her work.
Neighbors knew all was well when Grandmother was singing!
She was like a lark; quick, sleek and brown, caring about the
chicks in her nest.
Oh, how I long to be in that nest once more, just for a visit.
"Mommy," I hear a small voice, "Mommy, come!" that call was
meant for me. How could it be?
When I look into the mirror, I see a brown face like light brown
bread with wrinkles at its sides and arms much bigger than
yesterday, I am sure. I hope that my embrace is that of a cloud
and my eyes are hard to see, because I am tall.

I am 5 foot 3.

This poem came much later, however it is a perfect description
of the woman. She was this light brown small bundle of energy, much
like the plain little meadowlark, which astonishes one with the most

melodious song pouring from its puny grey brown body. So much so that he who has been lucky enough to witness the concert of a meadowlark will never forget its sound, even though the artist will have remained invisible, for its quite shy and prefers to blend into the foliage.

Now it's summer and Granny makes it a weekly task to check on some of her older friends. When Angelika goes along with her it is often quite boring, so she takes a book along to read, while Gran is ministering to her friends and neighbors. She never goes without a little gift of fruit or homemade jam or currant and blackberry juice extracted just recently from the bounty of the woods Grandpa hauls into the kitchen on a regular basis during the season.

"Those juices have healing power!" she would declare while pouring a glass full for one of her subjects, waiting patiently while they were struggling to drink the often sour or bitter brew.

Angelika did not like them much herself, they were nasty and as far as she was concerned not very palatable medicine.

If a person was too far gone to eat and drink, Granny would just sit with them, quietly read the paper, or if she sensed that the monotonous reading was annoying the person, just hold their hand. It seemed that she knew exactly what each person needed by a gesture or a frown or just the wrinkling of a sweaty brow. Angelika observed this well and was often asked to do the same; hold a hand or read from the good book while Granny was busy making tea or heating soup.

She remembered the sticky feeling when sweat was oozing from the skin of the dying person that she had intruded upon in the hospital. She remembered the feeling of thin skin stretched tightly over a waxy hand with empty veins and the bluish tint of cheeks and lips. She hated that smell that no amount of washing and disinfecting can hide.

After one of those visits she told Granny, that the neighbor Ann, they had just visited, would not live til morning. Gran stopped her vigorous pace and looked at her with some surprise.

"And how, my dear, do you think you know this? You better be very careful not to spread rumors that can get you into deep trouble."

"I could feel it in her hand," Angelika replied calmly. She had felt her own pulse, the regular steady beating of her heart, to recognize the difference.

"When I held her hand, her heartbeat was weak like the fluttering of a butterfly's wing and sometimes it stopped altogether, just to flutter again after a few seconds."

Angelika continued with her observations:

"There was no strength left in her and when I closed my eyes, I could hear the rustling of wings at the head of her bed. At first I stood up and looked outside to find the large birds. Seeing nothing, I decided that it had to be the wings of angels waiting to take her home!"

At this point Granny stopped walking completely. She took Angelika's face into both of her hands, and peered into that pinched little face with its serious brown eyes. Raising her voice, she said:

"Do not speak of this to anybody, they will think you're daft or touched. Most likely you are hanging around us old folk too much."

Grandmother was not surprised when a phone call in the morning told her that their neighbor, Ann, had peacefully died during the night.

And so it continued. Angelika was often afraid to touch a person's hand, afraid of what it might tell her. She decided to stay in the background during those visits to the sick with Granny. A few weeks later Gran was summoned to one of Grandpa's old friends, who was seriously ill, thought to be dying and had requested some of Granny's special tea. They wasted no time, finding the poor man nearly unconscious in his bed, his head lying high on a few pillows to ease his ragged breathing and his family standing weeping around him. Granny got busy in the kitchen and Angelika cowered in the back of the room, when the wife of the dying noticed her:

"Come closer, honey", she whispered, "talk to him! He always loved your company; especially your singing, come closer, hold his hand and sing the little snowflake song he liked so much. I don't think, he will ever see snow again."

With that she broke down weeping and pulled Angelika closer to the bedside. There she placed her hands on the folded pale ones on the blanket. Angelika stared at the bony grey head and sunken face and softly started to sing about the little snowflake who lives far away in the clouds:

"Schneefloeckchen, Weissroeckchen, wann kommst du geschneit, du lebst in den Wolken, dein Weg ist so weit."

Just as she was starting the second verse about how the lovely snowflake makes flowers, leaves and stars on the windowpane:

"Schneefloeckchen Weissroeckchen, du herzlicher Stern, malst Blumen und Blaetter. Wir haben dich gern."

The man's eyes popped open and a slow smile circled his sunken lips, just to disappear as fast as it had brightened his grave face. After she was done singing, Angelika noticed the steady rhythm of the man's pulse under her fingers. It had been there all along, she just did not notice it while she was concentrating on the words. Besides the steady pulse his hand was pale but warm, no sticky sweat, no flutter just an even beat, promising life.

"Oh, how he loved your singing," the man's wife exclaimed, hugging Angelika tightly and kissing her on the cheek.

"Thank you thank you, you dear little girl!"

The minute the wife's lips had touched her face, Angelika felt something like a shockwave coursing through her. She felt a weakness in the woman's body and when she hugged her close, the scent of sweet and nauseating decay filled her nostrils.

'It just can't be,' she thought, 'she is not the one we were called to see. It must be because she has been too busy caring for the sick one that she has not had time to wash or change.'

Trying to hide her surprise and her revulsion, she quickly freed herself of the old woman's embrace to find Granny in the kitchen preparing her special tea with the well-known healing power.

"What is it, child?" Granny had noticed the sickly pallor of her face and was worried.

"We have to go home, Gran, I don't feel well!" Angelika mumbled.

"Ok darling, let me give them the tea and we will go, I will explain, that you are tired." Granny was taking the tray into the sickroom, thinking: 'I cannot take this child with me anymore. She is just getting to sensitive.'

The old man had gone back to sleep and was unable to drink his tea at this time. Granny made their excuse and holding Angelika's hand set off towards home.

"Are you really sick?" she asked.

"No, not really, I just had to get away from that house and those poor clueless people."

"But why, what was different?" Granny was perplexed.

"You did not see him smile, Granny? He smiled when I sang the snowflake song."

"What's so strange about that? He always liked your singing."

"Oh, but I could not stand it any longer, the others were sitting around the bed, sad and waiting and Granny, he is not going to die. They are sitting around the wrong one."

"What do you mean by that, in God's name?"

They had stopped walking, because Granny wanted to get to the bottom of this strange conversation. Angelika was looking down at her sturdy brown leather shoes she hated with a passion, not wanting to catch Gran's eye.

"It's her, Granny. It's she who is going to die!"

And then she started to cry. Granny was seriously disturbed now. Up to this point Angelika's forebodings and feelings were nothing out of the ordinary. She, herself, could see and often knew with certainty when a person was nearing his end. Until now she had ascribed it to her overwrought imagination and fascination with disease and death, but this was different. She took the cold little hands into hers and said:

"Angelika dear, I know you have those feelings, I get them too and sometimes when things we thought or dreamed of come true, it can be scary, but it's usually nothing but good old common sense combined with intuition and often just plain coincidence. So, cheer up, we are going home and you will forget about all this for right now."

Angelika thought that that was a good idea until three days later, when the news had gotten around, that the dying man was quite recovered and his healthy wife was found dead in bed. Apparently she had been ill for some time, but did not worry about herself, since her husband was dying.

Chapter 3

Bella

This latest occurrence required a visit to one of Gran's oldest friends, Bella from Bohemia, whom some considered a real live witch. Grandma and Bella had a lot in common. They were both refugees. While most of Gran's family had survived the war, Bella's did not. Her husband fell during the Second World War and her parents and all her children, except her oldest daughter, had died of starvation and disease in a refugee camp. After all, German nationals had to be evicted from their Czechoslovakian home.

She lost her country, her house and watched her younger children starve to death under the watchful eye of Russian guards. She had survived abuse most cannot imagine directed towards her and what was even worse for Bella, towards her oldest daughter. They survived because she gave in to Russian soldiers; her body and soul in exchange for a crust of bread.

The daughter married right after the war. They bought the house next door. The young couple lived downstairs and Bella moved into the little apartment upstairs. Perhaps the daughter blamed Bella for not being able to protect her, perhaps she just had to hide her feelings and harden her heart to survive. It was obvious even to ten year-old Angelika, that there was no love lost between mother and daughter.

Bella had moved into two tiny rooms upstairs. There was a small kitchen and a bathroom without heat and running hot water. After Bella's grandson was born, Angelika used to visit often to help Bella with the baby while both parents worked.

She could never understand how anybody could live with such few possessions. After all her grandparents were refugees too, but their place was nicely furnished and comfortable. Granny had many pretty things around her and they all had nice clothes.

Bella's place was barren. A coal stove in the living room and a cook stove in the kitchen provided heat. The kitchen had a cupboard, a table and two chairs, the wood box near the stove became extra seating when needed. The living room appeared empty with a horse-hair stuffed ancient settee, a single chair, a lamp and a radio. There were no curtains on the windows. They were not needed, for every available window and wall space was taken up by many different bundles of drying herbs, spices and fruits. The whole place seemed to be a combination of apothecary and fruit cellar. Angelika thought it heavenly! The scent did not only come from all the walls and windows, but was especially potent in the kitchen where pots and cauldrons bubbled and steamed with all kinds of interesting potions and infusions. It was always the warmest spot in the apartment.

With all windows veiled in mist Bella, Granny and Angelika often sat at the table happily sipping some delicious teas which sometimes looked suspiciously red or green. While Gran and Bella talked, Angelika used to grow quite sleepy, but never drifted too far as not to hear the stories of deportation and suffering. She never got tired of the tales, no matter how often they were repeated. Because it was adult material, she pretended not to listen and busied herself with the baby, while secretly storing all the stories in her mind for a careful examination later.

Bella knew all about herbs and flowers and what to do with roots and how to dry mushrooms. Grandpa and she had many discussions about the varieties and safety of the different kinds. Some were quite poisonous when consumed raw, but could be boiled, then eaten safely while the remaining water could be used to treat certain illnesses when dosed correctly. Bella new the exact doses for many cures. While Grandpa was knowledgeable, he respected Bella's gift and wisdom. No wonder people thought her strange, and most kept their distance for while they mocked her, they feared her more.

Angelika often had a hard time dealing with the nasty, gossipy tongues of the townspeople. Bella was her friend and she was not affected by her strangeness or her eccentric appearance. Bella sewed, knitted and crocheted her own clothes. Nobody knew her real age, which was difficult to guess. She always looked the same; small in stature, thin as a reed with a good size hump she proudly carried between her shoulder blades. One would have thought her ancient, but her quick movements, sharp eyes and mind betrayed that thought. Her hair was white and clustered in curly abundance around her narrow head. She restrained it into a tight bun on the back of her head, but the boiling pot and steaming kettle on her stove provided too much moisture to keep it straight and confined. Many tendrils escaped and wound around her rosy face, framing sharp little twinkly blue eyes and a generous mouth which laughed often showing her own strong yellow teeth. Her nose and chin were prominent and the little hairy wart on the tip of her chin bounced happily up and down when she talked. She always wore the same thing; a long cotton skirt, blouses and various homemade sweaters depending on the time of year. When she was not busy in winter, she made her own jewelry out of fine gold and silver wire. She wound it tightly over little frames creating broaches and hangers depicting butterflies, flowers and leaves. It was a folk-art handed down through generations from her people in Bohemia.

Angelika loved to listen to her stories, while her own daughter appeared to be ashamed of Bella's strange ways and the neighborhood feared her, but Angelika was fascinated. Once the grandson had outgrown his crib, the daughter decided that a daycare situation would be more appropriate for her son. Granny and Angelika thought it outrageous, not only for depriving Bella of her grandson, but for the loss the little boy suffered by not being raised by his gifted grandmother. After the deed was done, Angelika sat with Bella, sipping tea and when she was trying to console her, Bella informed her, that it was time for her to move into her own place. She said a little house quite appropriate for her had become available at the edge of the forest. She said that she was able to afford the rent and she would finally be away from her son-in-law, who was not unhappy about her leaving. Angelika could not believe her ears:

"But you will be all alone! What happens if you're sick? And how will I be able to visit you all the time?"

"First of all, dear child, I am never sick, and I am not that far away, that you will not be able to drop in any time you want. Once I show you the way, it will take you no time on your bike!"

Soon after that conversation the moving truck arrived and very quickly Bella's few belongings got packed in and off they went. It was a very sad day for Angelika and her family who had grown to love that old woman. The apartment was now empty. No more steamed-up windows and herbal mists drifting across the yard towards Angelika's house. The dark soulless windows now stared bleakly into the garden as if they if they were veiled in mourning.

It did not take long when workmen arrived at the scene to remodel and modernize the place for it to be in move-in condition for new and better paying customers. Curtains and blinds appeared at all windows, which were now never opened. A young, bland couple moved in. They were strangers to the town and shyly moved in and out of the building in a hurried pace like mice, who did not want to divulge the whereabouts of their nest.

The neighborhood was not the same without Bella and those freshly painted and curtained windows were silent witnesses of Angelika's dismay. After a couple of weeks had passed, Gran thought that it was the proper time to visit Bella in her new home at the edge of the forest. Sunday was a beautifully bright and sunny early fall day. The air was crisp, the sky cerulean blue without a cloud, when they set out right after lunch, to look for early fall mushrooms and then check on Bella on their way back.

"If we get lucky, Bella can share in our bounty!" said Granny.

Angelika was not too thrilled. She did not like looking for mushrooms. One had to go off the path deep into the woods and con-centrate on the ground, where they were hiding among low growing grasses and moss. One had to look carefully or miss them altogether. You had to bend down and with a clean knife cut them off their stem to preserve the root system so more would grow after the next rain. It was tedious and boring hard work. Angelika liked to skip and run; mushroom picking was for old and slow people, not for her. It was almost as bad as gathering berries; blueberries being the worst, because of their size it took forever to fill a bucket. And one did not leave until the bucket was full. The reward was not so great either, the first few tasted good, but afterwards they got to be bland and mushy. One had to add lots of sugar and lemon juice to revive their taste. Granny used them mostly fresh on pancakes or in compotes, declaring them a healthy treat. Angelika did not think that it made up for the backbreaking and boring labor.

But right now it was fall, time for mushrooms, time for the tastier varieties than the ones in spring. They got lucky and their bag was soon full. Now it was time to look for Bella's new house.

When they walked around the bend of the deserted woody path, they came up to a very small wooden shed.

"This cannot be right!" exclaimed Angelika "This is so small and rough, no person could be comfortable there!" It really was more of a hut than a proper house. A solid wooden shed with a red tiled roof.

"Well, at least the roof looks sound," said Gran.

A red brick chimney puffed bilious white smoke into the blue sky. There was a window on each side of the hut. Old fashioned ancient glass with its imperfect bubbles and streaks broke the light like a wavy prism. As they got closer to the property, they saw a small fenced in garden, where a stuck-up rooster, guarding a few hens, proudly stalked around and noisily announced that strangers were on the premises. They stopped short of the fence and took time to admire this peaceful setting of hut, chickens and flower garden. Angelika exclaimed:

"This looks exactly like the witch's candy house in Hansel and Gretel! The wood looks like chocolate and the windows like spun sugar. The roof could be red licorice!"

"Well, should we start singing:

Knusper, knusper knaeuschen, wer knabbert an meinem Haeuschen,

(Chomp, chomp, crunch, who is nibbling on my house)

"Or should we just knock like normal people?"Gran was having fun with Angelika's imagination. Just then the door opened and Bella was standing in the wooden doorway with a huge smile on her lips.

"My favorite friends, come in, I don't need an alarm, I have my buddy Red, here," she was pointing at the rooster, who still agitated, had jumped on the roof of the chicken coop for a better vantage point.

They were let into a large kitchen looking much like the old one. Again Bella used wood to cook and heat. Many dried weeds and leaves decorated windows and walls and her cauldron was happily bubbling away. On a pillow on top of the rocking chair purred a huge black cat lazily opening its blazing green eyes for a quick look at the intruders, just to go back to sleep, curling himself into an even tighter bundle.

'All she needs is a crow,' thought Angelika. 'The cat? The cauldron? It's a good thing we know her so well or, perhaps, we don't know her as well as we think.'

Bella shooed the cat off the chair.

"This one stood by my door in the morning after I moved in and told me, that this was his house first, but if I played my cards right, he would let me stay here for a while. It was rough going at first, because he thought himself the boss and me the intruder. Once he realized he did not have to depend solely on his mouse hunting skills to survive and accepted a few tasty morsels from my stove, we decided on this living arrangement. He tolerates me and I don't tell him what to do. So far it's been working out. Although he is a free spirit and has a tendency to disappear for days only to walk back in, expecting a meal of roasted chicken and a thorough petting!"

At this point the black cat had stretched himself in front of the stove, his paws stretched out in front of him and his bright green eyes never wavering from Bella's face at her account of their meeting as if he understood every word.

'She sure has a way with all creatures,' thought Angelika.

It was cozy and warm and peaceful, watching the cat close his eyes and while she was drowsily listing to the contented murmur between Gran and Bella, she also fell fast asleep while the rocker gently swayed. A while later Gran shook her shoulder, saying:

"It's time to go, Grandpa will want his supper."

Angelika hated to leave this cozy place and promised to come back soon to visit.

"Any time is fine," said Bella, "if I am out, just let yourself in, the place is never locked, and I would not be gone for long."

Chapter 4
Coming of Age

Their visits continued for years. While Bella never seemed to get any older, Angelika blossomed into a fine young girl of seventeen.

Now she had to make a decision about her future. Her primary education was coming to an end and since the family was poor, further schooling was not an option. Still fascinated by herbs and potions, loving the smell of the local apothecary and drug stores, she wanted nothing more than to study pharmacy; alas, there was no money for years of university studies. She had many talks about her future calling with Bella. While most girls and especially most boys Angelika's age were silly creatures, she had a few close friends with whom she was able to commiserate about their future plans.

Those earlier experiences at the sickbeds of her grandparent's elderly friends had frightened her to the point of avoiding physical contact with them. She thought it was quite safe around her friends, who were all young and happy and appeared as indestructible as she. She talked to Bella about her fears. Her advice was:

"You have a gift, you will learn to use it, don't let it frighten you, perhaps someday you will be able to change someone's destiny."

That was easier said than done.

'To change someone's destiny?'

How Angelika was to figure that out remained a mystery for now.

It all became clear the following winter. There had been a hard freeze for several weeks, the river had flooded the fields and both were solidly frozen, making it possible for the people to ice skate on the smooth surface between the silenced damn and the large iron bridge in the center of the town. Angelika did not have skates and would not get any, because Gran never trusted the mayor's proclamation, that the ice was safe.

"This is a wide river with a swift current, deep enough to transport barges, it will never be safe! Stay away!"

Angelika usually listened and remained obedient; however, the short cut across the river on her way to school was a temptation. While the boys and girls frolicked on the ice and danced on shiny skates over glittering surfaces in the rusty winter sunsets, their voices reverberating from the depth of the river up to the bridge, where Angelika stood looking longingly at the spectacle below, another girl joined her saying:

"What I would give to be down there."

Angelika knew her fairly well. She was a couple years younger, the only child of an older couple, who lived not too far away from her grandparents.

"I know what you mean; I am not allowed to be there either!"

"Oh well, let's go and get a coke, that will make us feel better!"

Having said that, the girl grabbed her arm and started to pull her along playfully off that bridge to go to the little snack bar where the kids used to meet.

Angelika could feel the girl's thin arm through the winter jacket and had the strangest sensation. The girl turned to face her and she could see her heart-shaped little face framed by shiny dark curls peeking out from under her cap. Her strikingly hazel eyes with black stripes had locked with Angelika's smiling brown ones, shooting sparks out from even blacker pupils, when Angelika noticed an electric current shooting up her arm, across her shoulder right into the middle of her chest, making her momentarily breathless.

"Are you alright?"

The girl let go of her hand.

"You look funny!"

"Oh sure, it's nothing, I got shocked, must be static electricity, did you not feel it?"

"No, I felt nothing; you're silly, let's go!"

With one last look at the merry skaters, they took off to get that coke. Afterwards they walked home together and Angelika had forgotten all about that incident until the following week.

The weather had suddenly turned milder, like it often does at the end of January. The sun was shining brightly and the ice on the river started to creak and moan like it was fighting to give in and away to the demands of the current. The river's edge turned marshy and after a few days of moaning and creaking, the ice cracked. First small, then larger crevices appeared with black icy water churning underneath. The boys made a sport of it called 'floe jumping'. Angelika had only tried it once and still felt guilty about keeping it a secret from Granny. Ever since, she had promised herself never to do it again, no matter how exciting it still looked.

It was a Saturday. School had just let out at noon, when the news, a little girl had drowned in the icy river, travelled swiftly across town. Angelika did not have to ask who? She just knew. Before Granny could think of a consoling word, she snatched her coat from the wardrobe and dashed down the street, across the field and through the woods to Bella's hut.

Bella had hung out her clothes to freeze dry as usual and was in the process of carefully removing stiff skirts and stockings from the line. From far away it looked like she was fighting with large flapping flat people. The sleeves of the shirts were flung wide as if protesting in terror, the skirts a solid shield and the stockings hung straight, kicking the wind as if they were objecting to the torture of freeze drying. If Angelika had not been so disturbed and upset, she would have thought the scene amusing. Since Bella's vision was clouded by cataracts, which she denied, she could not recognize the runner at that distance, until Angelika had nearly flung herself into her arms and started to sob.

"Slow down child!"

Bella was trying to see her face while holding on to the stubborn laundry at the same time.

"Let's get into the house first, let me put this down, what has you so upset, my dear?"

They tumbled, Bella, Angelika and the shirts, in a heap into the warm hut. Angelika collapsed into the rocking chair, sending the cat screeching into the corner.

"You just won't believe what happened!" she sobbed, "My friend drowned in the river today and I knew it. I knew it!"

"How on earth could you have known about it?" asked Bella carefully.

In between sobs and cries she told Bella the whole story of how she and her little friend were watching the kids ice-skating from the bridge, when the girl grabbed her arm and she started to feel shocks traveling all the way up to her chest.

"First of all," Bella crooned, "you did not know it, all you did was feel her energy, perhaps some static. One always has static with this newfangled material called poly-something that they make everything out of, even coats. Worthless stuff, if you ask me, there is no warmth in it what-so-ever!"

"But Bella, I believe it was the same thing as before! I was scared and just did not want to recognize it. Perhaps I could have stopped her! But how?"

While Angelika was reconstructing the events for Bella and tried to understand her role in all of it, Bella made herself busy at the stove. She poured water into a pan and a few seeds, and when the water was boiling, she added a few leaves and a pinch of this-and-that from her drying bins. Soon an interesting aroma filled the little room. She filled a large mug by pouring the mixture through a sieve and after adding a spoonful of honey, handed the mug to the girl with the command:

"No more words, let's sip and have a good think!"

It was one of Bella's favorite lines. As Angelika was bringing the cup to her nose she thought, 'this tea is different from all the others, she has ever made for me. The taste was bitter, yet sweet and sour at the same time. How is it possible?'

There was a component which excited each individual taste bud at once. It prickled her tongue but was smooth in her throat. After a few sips she felt a calming sensation pass through her brain, her limbs felt heavy and weightless and everything seemed to have shifted. A feeling of warmth spread from her stomach throughout her body, the sensation of floating became more pronounced and just as she was starting to question whether she should safely enjoy this state or panic, she fell asleep.

Chapter 5

The Dream

Angelika awoke. Startled she jumped up.

"Oh my God, Bella, how late is it, its dark outside, how long did you let me sleep? Gran will be worried to death."

She pulled the blanket from around her shoulders, straightened her limbs which had gone to sleep and were now tingling as she was attempting to stand up. Her head was spinning and she had to hold on to the rocking chair for balance. Once her eyes had focused, she realized that this was not Bella's hut anymore. The chair and some of the furnishings were similar but her surroundings had definitely changed. It was a much larger room with wooden cots and night-stands and strange looking dressers all around. There was no Bella and she started to panic.

'Where in God's name am I?'

"What happened?" she asked herself.

Everything had changed. There was a large iron stove in the middle of the room with wisps of yellow smoke billowing from its crevices. Angelika coughed and wiped her face. By now her eyes were not tearing from the smoke alone, but from sheer fright.

"Hello, is anybody here? Where am I? Is somebody going to answer me?"

Once she found her sea legs, she scanned the room. It was really a hall, having nothing in common with Bella's cozy hut.

'This must be a bad dream,' she thought as she started to pinch her face and arms til it hurt. Alas, she was awake and there was no escape!

Her hands looked like her hands, small with chewed-up finger-nails and ragged nail beds. As she pulled the sleeves of her blouse up, she felt and saw the red marks on her arms from her pinching. This certainly was not her shirt. It was gauzy and stiff with tight cuffs around her wrists. As her eyes wandered down her person, she noticed the long blue skirt made from the same stiff material, reaching down all the way to her ankles which were sticking in black sturdy boots with more eyelets than she had ever seen on a shoe for a tight fit. 'No wonder I could not find my legs under all that garb,' she thought. Her waist felt tight; circled by a broad white band crossing her back and forming a starched white bib across her chest, creating the apron that covered the stiff blue dress.

"Where are my jeans?" she cried, "And my polo shirt, it was brand new. What is this get up, starched and stiff? I feel weird! Even my head feels wrong. Oh God, what's on my head? Where is my hair?"

Franticly she reached up, feeling for her long hair, her crowning glory. As she patted her neck she noticed a starched collar and reaching up, she felt the cool hard brim of a stiff cap. She realized that she was wearing a cap with her thick wavy hair pinned under it.

"I need a mirror!"

As she was taking in her new surroundings with the many bedsteads, night stands and dressers, she spotted one. It was a half-length mirror with a few cracks and quite clouded with age, but she had no difficulty recognizing the image. An old-fashioned nurse wearing her eyes, her nose and mouth, forehead and hands was staring back at her with a frightened wide-eyed expression. Looking closer and closer until her breath clouded the image, peering deeply into her eyes, she tried to find her own person.

Suddenly a loud and laughing voice pulled her out of her astonishment!

"Hey, what have we here? You're beautiful enough for this place!"

She quickly moved away from the mirror and turned around. Expecting to now wake up and apologizing for this Halloween outfit, she saw a tall young man approaching with a wide open smiling face and blue eyes crinkled up with mirth.

"I am sorry, I don't belong here," she managed, pulling at her dress and apron, "I don't quite know what this is all about. I went to sleep and when I woke up, I was here and this is all too weird!"

"Well," he said, "you are here and that's what it's all about, nothing else matters. We were expecting you!"

"Expecting me? You don't even know me!"

"That's quite right, I don't yet, but we must change that in a hurry! We must! How impolite of me."

With two big steps he was by her side, grabbing her hand with both of his and shaking it, he said:

"Where are my manners? I am Merlin, James Merlin, the famous Doctor Merlin."

When he was done shaking her hands, he put his arm around her shoulder and laughed, "Well, at least that was my father, the famous Dr. Merlin; you can just call me James!"

"I am Angelika, and I still don't know why I am dressed like this?"

At that he looked at her somewhat puzzled. "What do the nurses and sisters wear where you come from?"

"Nurses? Wait a minute. You think I am a nurse?"

Before she could explain herself, he thundered: "Well, it does not matter, you are here and I will introduce you to Sister Anna, our dear Matron."

"The matron, what matron? But I don't know anything!"

"Oh, don't you worry. You will do, you will do just fine and she will love you!"

"I doubt that very much, once she finds out!"

James took her arm and pulled her along past all those empty bedsteads into a little alcove where several other girls dressed much like her were seated around an older quite severe, but not unkind looking woman, dressed all in black with the same kind of head-covering, minus the apron.

"Sister Anna, look what I found sleeping back there in the rocking chair."

Angelika stood with her head down, afraid to look up, afraid to reconcile with this new reality. Everybody stopped what they were doing, rolling bandages and cutting gauze from big bales, to get a good look at the new one. Sister took a ruler from her desk and lifted Angelika's chin up to study her face.

"So you're the one they told us about!"

'I wished somebody would have told me,' thought Angelika. As she looked up, she saw the white face of the older nurse with her tired but kind eyes and felt a little better. Soon the other girls gathered around her.

"Hi, I am Elsa!"

"I am Rose."

"My name is Dora and this is Maria!"

"I am Angelika!" she said quietly, "And I still don't know why I am here!"

"None of us know," shouted Elsa, "we are all new sisters and this is a new hospital. The old one got overcrowded!"

Angelika looked around. She was quite familiar with hospitals, remembering the time she had spent there visiting Granny. She remembered vividly the clean white tiles, white iron bedsteads, clean linen and the smell of disinfectants not to mention the nurses in their casual whites, neat hairdos under sparkling white caps, wearing hospital clogs and lab coats.

"Yes, yes," Rose chimed in, "this is really quite modern. There are curtains in between the bed-stands; each nightstand has its own special place for bedpans and basins. And we have our own station, right over there from where we can see all the beds and observe the patients!"

"But this is not modern!" cried Angelika. "With that beastly stove in the middle, all the poor patients are going to choke to death. How are we supposed to use oxygen with an open flame in the room? This is really screwy, after all this is 1967."

After this last outburst all five of them and Dr. James stared at her in a strange way.

"My goodness, girl," said Matron, "you must have really been worn out to sleep so deeply that you got your numbers mixed up. This is 1679. And about the oxygen, we get that from our windows. That's why they are mostly open. The Doctor believes in plenty of that, as a matter of fact. All patients get an air bath every morning, even in the dead of winter. When it is freezing out, all the patients get covered up and are instructed to breathe deeply in and out through their noses only. In summer when it's hot, we lay them half-naked on their sheets and the windows are open all the time."

Angelika kept quiet, just hoping to wake up in Bella's hut any minute now, and for this nightmare to be over.

'1679, what the hell? I just want to know what is screwing with me,' she thought. 'It had to be that strange tasting tea.'

As much as she tried to concentrate and wish herself back into her familiar century, it was to no avail. Once she peeked into that mirror above the dresser, an old-fashioned nurse looked back, grinning at her, an impish nose and widened lips baring little white teeth.

"I guess that's it then, at least for a little while," said Angelika looking at the expectant faces surrounding her. She set her jaw and gave in. "1679 it is."

Chapter 6

Rats

"Come on Angelika, we will show you our room and introduce you to our other roommates, Maria and Dora!"

Elsa and Rose took her by her hands, pulling her up and out of the strange hall into a dark and dank hallway leading up a few flights of rickety steps into what appeared to be a type of dormitory. There were two small windows peeking out over the red clay tiled roofs of half-timbered houses of an unfamiliar medieval town. Along the walls stood six beds much like the small cots she had noticed in the ward earlier. A large oil lamp stood in the middle of the table giving off a dim light and more smoke than necessary. A single candle decorated each night stand.

"You must burn the candle sparingly, Matron only gives us two per week," said Rose.

"Most of our reading has to be done during the day."

A small chest, standing at the foot of each cot with its lid open, finished the furnishings.

"Great," said Angelika, "no electricity, reading with candle light or that stinking oil lamp, no closets… Where are we supposed to put our clothes?"

Four pairs of eyeballs stared at her outburst with incredulity. Their owners had absolutely no idea what she was worrying about.

Elsa was the first to respond. "In the chest, silly! We don't have much; our underclothes, a Sunday dress, and a workday dress, that's about it. All our uniforms are hung up at the door and we will get a new apron every day and a fresh dress once a week."

"Once a week, a new dress? You have got to be kidding me, they must smell great on Saturday and there is probably no deodorant."

"What's deodorant?" Elsa asked.

"You put it under your armpits after you take a shower. It's made from baking soda and some gel and aluminum and perfume."

"Never heard of it!

"What's a shower?"

All eyes stared at her once again in disbelief.

"Where are your bathrooms and the toilets?" Angelika was getting desperate.

There was still no reaction from the starring gallery. Finally after she made the shape of a tub, the sign of water, the shape of a hose attached to a vessel, and squatted down pretending to use the bathroom, it clicked:

"Oh, you mean the privy. That's outside right next to the water pump!" Elsa was bending over gurgling with laughter. "We bring in a bucket of water and heat it on the stove. Check under your stand, there is a basin, you empty the pitcher and voila, there is your bathroom. Once a week we heat water and fill the big tub and wash everything, you know, just before we get our clean dress."

While Angelika could not believe her ears, they were baffled by her simpleness. Elsa noticing her distress, declared:

"Listen, we have so much fun, we make it a party. A curtain fits around the tub for privacy, don't worry!"

'Fun,' thought Angelika, 'we will all be smoky, stinky and tired. Besides I cannot imagine sleeping in a room with four other people.'

While Rose and Elsa were explaining routine things to this simpleton, who strangely did not have any clues about daily living, Maria flung herself onto her bed, contemplating why this very strange girl was popped into their midst.

'What a weirdo!' she thought. 'She looks at everything as if she has never encountered it before. Her speech is different, somewhat more refined and yet she seems to know of things, like oxygen which comes from a tube and is connected to a large reservoir.'

It was puzzling for everyone!

Maria was dark and pretty with chestnut colored hair and fiery eyes with a sleek stature, much like Angelika. She felt acute competition; for she was used to being the pretty one, the smart one, the quick catch, and proudly praised by both her parents and teachers.

"Well, bring it on," she mumbled. "We will find out who is the smart one and the pretty one around here."

With that she pulled herself up and checked her face in the mirror of her night stand, studying the perfect skin, the gentle curve of her neck, her straight nose and her heavily lashed dark eyes. So reassured she felt quite superior at that moment.

Meanwhile Dora was busy putting her things into the chest at the bottom of the bed. She folded her underclothes neatly into even piles before stashing them away. She appeared neat and uncomplicated. She knew that she was plain, built like a boy, straight up and down. Her three brothers were always teasing her about her large and unfeminine figure. Always teasing her by saying that God forgot to give her 'lady bumps,' she should have really been another boy. She would laugh it off:

"You just wait until I grow up, I will get breasts and I have strength so I can continue to beat you guys at all your games!"

So she waited for breasts which never appeared and hips which never widened. She was given instead; a cool head, a sharp brain and a great sense of humor. She was smart, strong, kind and felt absolutely not a shred of jealousy towards her more feminine and rounder friends. As a matter of fact, sometimes she thought she could love them. But that is a different story, neither here or there.

While Rose was trying to calm Angelika, Elsa was adding a few pieces of wood to the fire in the little round potbelly stove which was heating their room.

"I will make us all a cup of tea," she announced as she checked the kettle, added some more water from the pitcher and busied herself with cups and sugar.

Just then Angelika noticed the cabinet behind the stove. There were earthen mugs and plates and some very strange looking silverware. The knives and forks were chunky and felt heavy when she was weighing them in her hands.

"Let's set out mugs and get the sugar bowl. There is no milk, but we will make do!"

Elsa seemed clearly to be in charge. She appeared to be the oldest.

'She has to be at least twenty-five,' thought Angelika. She was an imposing figure of a girl, quite large boned with a broad face and the most endearing smile, all of which made Angelika feel quite safe.

Elsa's people were farmers who had worked their land for generations. Nothing seemed too complicated for her. She was calm and capable, and could deliver a calf just as easily as a human baby. She bragged about having helped with the birth of eight of her siblings. She, being the oldest of twelve children, found it quite natural to be her mother's assistant in everything. Through her eyes life was simple; birthing, working, dying. Everything in-between is just what it is destined to be, no use getting too excited, just go with the flow and hope for the best.

Angelika understood immediately that Elsa's simple approach; her country good sense mingled with an infinite amount of kindness and good will would make her the perfect nurse and care-giver; not to mention her sheer physical strength, which would come in handy with some of the sicker patients. Later she witnessed how Elsa's large but deft hands could not only lift a large man, but could also caress an infant's burning forehead with utmost gentleness. Right now Elsa poured boiling water over the tea leaves into an old brown earthenware pot and closed the lid.

"Three minutes, no longer!" she commanded, "Or the black leaves lose their punch and the drink will put us all to sleep!"

"Yes, Mother Superior," piped Rose, who had perched herself on the edge of Dora's bed. "No more than three minutes," she mimicked Elsa's thunder voice.

"And when we are done with our tea, let's study the leaves."

"Oh, please Elsa, tell us our future!" Rose cried.

Once the tea was poured, the girls were hovering around the warm stove sipping contently from their mugs, when Angelika thought:

'Reading tea leaves, I have heard about it. Granny would not have approved that's for sure! She did not like any type of witchery, like palm readings or fortune-telling. To her it was a bad omen to dabble in magic, perhaps even blasphemous.'

"There is a reason, why a person is not to know the future!" She used to say. "That's up to God and God alone!"

Granny had developed a healthy respect for the occult because of a strange experience she had had many years ago. She often told the story of when, as a very young woman, she was going to the fair with several of her girlfriends. They all decided to have their fortune read by a gypsy in the colorful tent with the sun and the moon painted on the canvas flaps and the shining globe into which a strange bejeweled dark-haired witch of a woman was peering.

One by one they entered her tent; handing over their pennies and stretching out their palms in anticipation. Granny remembered that strange woman holding her hand, then stroking her skinny hairy forearms, the whole time muttering to herself. "So much hair," and after a minute or two, she peered into her eyes and said:

"See all that hair, you will be very rich someday and you will have three men in your life!"

At the time Granny thought this quite exciting, but realized much later how 'spot on' this gypsy had been. While she never had any money to speak of, Granny had always felt quite rich in mind and health and the three men proved to be her husband and her two sons. But now back to the tent.

All the girls, except the mayor's daughter, had been told some type of banality by the gypsy. When it was time for her to enter the tent the mood changed abruptly. The girl was very pretty and spoiled, so when the gypsy took her hand and hesitated, she got mad and shouted at the woman to hurry up. She called her a fool and a fraud and that she would not pay a penny for this nonsense. That's when Granny witnessed the gypsy grabbing the girls palm and looking directly into her eyes venomously declared that she would die before the year was done.

All the girls fled the tent, consoling the mayor's daughter and laughing it off. Unfortunately the gypsy was once again correct in her foresight. She had hesitated because of what she saw and she did not want to frighten the girl. Alas, before the year was done the girl had married the butcher's son in a great ceremony and died in childbirth nine months later. With the retelling of the story Granny had imposed a great respect for magic and for gypsies on Angelika.

The girls had crowded around her while she was telling Granny's story. Rose looked positively frightened.

"Perhaps your Gran just made it all up, to scare you away from gypsies!" she offered.

"You don't know my Granny, she would not tell it, if it were not so!"

Rose, who really looked like a rose, was the smallest one of them. Red curls framed a flawless face and large green eyes with impossible long lashes were brimming with tears:

"Well, perhaps we shall not read tea leaves today!"

"Nonsense, who cares about a dumb story, it's just for fun," hollered Elsa.

"Give me your cups girls! No, don't drain them all the way, leave just a few drops on the bottom, now swirl the leaves around three times, just like this! Now close your eyes and empty your mind! Stop, open your eyes and what do you see?"

Angelika stared at the bottom of her mug:

"It's just tea, nothing else!"

"Of course its tea leaves silly, what do you think? It did not turn into silver or gold. Tell me the shape they are forming in your cup."

Elsa's voice took on a serious tone.

"We will read the leaves in three stages; from the rim, the middle and from the base. Empty your minds, it is now very important to be calm and at peace."

Elsa voice continued to be low and soothing as she was giving her instructions slowly. At this point everyone had swirled their cups three times and was waiting with baited breath.

"Turn your cup so the handle will rest in your right hand and look at the configurations of the leaves carefully, starting clockwise at twelve o'clock. If a subject or a person enters your mind and cannot be easily dismissed; bear in mind that this may be what you are meant to see!"

Angelika stared with all her concentration at the shallow pool of tea at the bottom of her cup and at the slight splattering of different sizes of leaves gathered towards the rim and the sides.

"I think I see crosses. Yes, they are definitely crosses and flowers and a half moon or maybe a big J and a tree, and....."

"Wait a minute," cried Elsa, "do you really have all those things in your cup? I have to see this!"

"I have a cross too," whispered Rose, "and a bird, I am sure it's a bird!"

"I have boxes," said Dora.

"What? I have never seen boxes."

Elsa quickly scanned every cup, stopping at Maria's who had not swirled her last drop of tea, but had sat quietly observing everyone else.

"This is crazy behavior!" she said angrily. "I don't believe in this crap!"

With that outburst Maria jumped up and dumped the remainder of her tea into the waiting dishpan.

"It is just for fun, don't take it so seriously!" Elsa shouted, putting a soothing arm around Maria, who seemed genuinely upset.

"Don't worry, I will do the washing up and then we have another cup of tea!" she joked.

Elsa got up and as she was looking at the bottom of the dishpan, she cried out:

"Maria, come and look at your leaves!"

They all jumped up, staring at the bottom of the pan, there was the perfect pattern of a crucifix, actually of three crosses, but the crucifix in the middle was clearly outlined with the image of a body.

Angelika could not believe her eyes:

"This is all very strange! Crosses, bodies, birds and half moons, what does it all mean?"

Even Elsa was stunned into silence at this moment and seemed to lose her cool and composure. Quietly she said:

"It means change. There will be change for all of us. Not always does a cross mean death, it could be faith and renewal. Angelika, you had a moon, which could mean new beginnings."

"Maybe it was a big J for Dr. James," Dora joked, "after all it was he who found you sleeping."

Angelika's head was spinning.

'Yesterday was 1967 and I was a brand new nursing student. I had never worked or studied in a hospital before. Today is 1679. I am sitting in an ancient dormitory with a group of girls, claiming to be nurses, reading tea leaves by candle light.'

Out loud she said, "Let's get rid of those cups and listen to what Granny would say. "Do good, do not worry and let the future belong to God!"

"Finally a word of reason!" mumbled Maria. "This is all a bunch of crap and is really not too much fun." She was glaring at Elsa angrily. Then she walked over to her bed, flopped down on it and closed her eyes to shut out the world.

Angelika and Elsa got busy removing the last traces from the cups.

"I wash, you dry!" said Elsa.

Dora and Rose were quietly whispering about the birds they each had seen. "I think they were doves," said Rose. "Doves mean rebirth and peace. We can certainly live with that."

'Too bad I drank all that tea', thought Angelika. 'Now I have to pee and there is no plumbing. I hope I don't have to find the so-called privy by myself in this scary place. I am still not really sure if I am awake or dreaming. Are these really women or are they ghosts? They don't seem like anybody I have ever met before. No wonder! They are almost three hundred years old. If I tell them the truth, they will think I am crazy and I hate to see what the insane asylums look like around here, considering that this is the new hospital everyone is so proud of!'

'Oh God,' she prayed, 'I really need your help! Where is this leading? Are you giving me a test, an exam, I cannot possibly pass?'

Just as she was getting totally freaked out, little beads of sweat forming on her forehead and her armpits feeling sticky, Elsa gave her a big bear hug and shouted:

"Well, it's time that I show you around before it gets too dark. We will all have to use the outhouse and we will get more water for washing up."

She took Angelika's hand and holding it firmly pulled her into a long passageway to a wide flight of dark steps.

"Let's hurry," she said, "it gets pitch-black here at night."

"What do I do if I have to pee at night?"

"If you just have to pee, it's no problem at all, we have pots under our beds and we all use them, put the lid on them and forget about it until morning."

"Things are getting definitely worse!"

"Oh relax," laughed Elsa.

"What's a little pee among friends?"

Leaving the stairwell, they soon found themselves in a large courtyard with high walls surrounding it. To her right she noticed two small buildings, which seemed to be their destination.

"Here we are. The left one is for boys and this one is ours. It's nice and clean. We use old paper; rub it between our hands to make it soft and voila!"

Angelika was beside herself now: 'No real toilet paper!' Well she had used an outhouse before when visiting friends in a small village or camping, but for it to be the rule is not acceptable.

"What do you do when it gets really cold?" she worried.

"You do it faster, girl, that's all."

Elsa seemed not to notice how upset Angelika was getting. She cheerfully pointed to a pump on a fountain in the middle of the court yard:

"That's where we get our water. Let's fill the pitchers!"

She had grabbed both water jugs, so they would not have to do this dark walk again.

"Girl, you must have been really rich and been in a big fancy place where water was coming from pipes right into your house."

Angelika agreed:

"Water was coming from pipes right into sinks. It was warm in winter when the central heating was on, but just as icy as this in the summer. Then, we had to heat all our water on the stove just like you."

"It's a good thing you are not too spoiled then," answered Elsa good naturedly.

As they hurried along the passageway, Elsa burdened with the jugs of water and Angelika with her heavy heart, they noticed some large shadows slinking along the walls. It was getting quite dark and Angelika could barely make out the shapes of many furry low-slung bodies.

"Oh my God," she burst out, "Rats!"

Just then several of the creatures lifted their heads and looked up as if they had heard their names. Tiny bright flashing eyes assaulted the girls from all sides.

"Elsa, oh my God, I have never seen so many! Where did they come from? They were not here before!"

"It's the time of day, dusk; it's when they come out to feed." Elsa seemed unconcerned.

"But rats, they're dirty; they're filthy, now I am really scared!"

Elsa swung the bottles at the hurrying bodies, hollering, "Away with you miserable devils, run for your life!"

"They looked at us with creepy almost human eyes as if they understood."

"There you go again! Its rats, honey, they are everywhere, that's why we close the doors and don't keep food in the room. You have an amazing imagination; water and oxygen that come out of pipes, rats that understand! Who ever heard of that? We had rats everywhere on the farm, that's what the cats were for."

"But, Elsa, these are as big as cats. You will need tigers to get rid of them."

Trying to ignore the creatures they hurried along the pass-way which appeared now twice as long as before. With danger lurking all around, Angelika was too scared to look further at the fleeing shadows, but she could not help noticing, that there was an exact order in their approach. On their right, the creatures were running with them, while on their left, they were going into the opposite direction. Finally they reached the end of the passage where the great gate stood open the way they had left it.

"I can't wait to get out of here!" shouted Angelika. "This is really scary!"

Elsa put down the bottles and looking Angelika straight into her eyes, she said:

"Let's close this gate, remember when your mother said, close the door, or were you born in a barn? We need to keep the heat in and the creatures out!"

At this point Angelika was close to tears and shouted back:

"First of all, I did not have a mother and we never ever had rats. There were a few in town by the river, but the street sweepers and gardeners kept them in check."

"Well, it must have been a mighty fancy place where you come from."

Elsa was clearly losing her cool with this prissy stranger.

"No, not at all fancy, just no rats, period!"

After they shoved the gate closed, Angelika picked up one of the jugs and started up the steps, when she nearly tripped over something soft.

She started to scream and almost dropped the water:

"It's a dead one! My foot bumped into its still warm body, how gross!"

"Don't tell me that you are also afraid of dead rats."

Elsa had also put down her jug and bent over to examine the casualty further. Pushing it gently with her foot, she declared in a professional voice:

"It's dead alright, a big brown rat, the size of a small cat."

It was lying on its side, the bare curled tail and all fours stretched out. Elsa kept pushing at it with the tip of her leather boot.

"Oh please," said Angelika. "Stop it! We have to tell somebody to get rid of it."

"And who do you think is going to do that, perhaps Dr. James, your knight in shining armor?"

"Oh, I don't care who, just as long as it will be gone!"

While Elsa kept poking the rat with her boot, moving it slightly from its former position, she noticed a large puddle of blood spreading out beneath the rat's head.

"Look," she said. "That rat bled to death from its mouth. It vomited blood and then it died. How curious is that?"

"Perhaps it got squashed or mauled," offered Angelika.

"Well, it had to be something big, like a dog, but I don't see any bite-marks and her fur is not ruffled. This rat was not in a fight, it was sick!"

"Now it's a she, my God, Elsa, let's get out of here. We have to tell Matron or Dr. James!"

"Nonsense, we get rid of it ourselves; they will think we are silly bothering them with this!" Then Elsa added thoughtfully, "It is weird though, that rat died of internal bleeding, I am sure of it."

"You are the nurse, but now we have to hurry," cried Angelika.

"There is a meeting tonight when we get briefed on the arrival of the new patients in the morning, let's not be late!" Elsa reminded them.

'I cannot wait,' thought Angelika. 'Perhaps all this mystery will get cleared up somehow.'

"Perhaps we get to go home soon," she said out loud.

"Home? I don't think that's in the cards," said Elsa.

"How long did they tell you that your assignment will be?"

"What assignment?"

"This is the reason why we are all here. We all volunteered and gave up good positions to come here. Apparently there is an emergency."

'Oh God, this is getting more curious by the minute', thought Angelika. 'If I tell her, that I went to sleep three hundred years in the future in some cozy hut sipping tea, she will have me declared crazy or at least unstable.'

Out loud she said, "Elsa, it's time we get back so we can find out what it's all about."

Elsa resolutely grabbed both pitchers and marched with large strides ahead, while Angelika was running after her trying to keep up. Walking back up the steps, she recognized the hall way to the dorm room. The other three girls were sitting on Maria's bed reviewing nursing ledgers.

Maria was reading out loud:

"When the patient is too sick to get out of bed, it is easier for two people to change the sheets. While one person is standing on each side of the bed, the patient is first instructed about the procedure. He is asked to roll to one side of the bed. If he cannot accomplish that alone, he is gently rolled by both nurses. While one nurse is holding his shoulders and hips, aligned straight to one side, the other can now change the sheets. When one side is properly tucked in, the patient is gently rolled over the hump by both to the finished side, the dirty linen is then removed quickly, the clean sheets are tucked in firmly and without a wrinkle, for a single wrinkle if one has to lay on it for some time, can become as bothersome as a rock. That's why hospital beds have to be neat and tidy at all times."

Angelika was looking at the illustrations and the explanations and found it mostly to be common sense. The bathing procedure seemed pretty simple too; start on the top, work down, keep the water as clean and as warm as possible, work quickly and gently and cover the patient in between sponging. Applications of heat and cold were on the next page. Always provide a barrier between the patient's skin and the cold or hot compress. There was a whole chapter on nutrition, which was fairly self-explanatory. Elevate the patient's head, make him sit up as straight as possible to prevent choking. Never give a body liquid if he has trouble swallowing or is coughing.

"Oh, Bella, how I could use your help now," lamented Angelika under her breath. But then a little voice came into her head and whispered:

'Just you remember; you do know Bella's secrets, think hard and remember, think about her herbs and leaves and spices and dried fruits. Chamomile for the stomach, willow bark for fever, linden-blossoms for colds, flu and bronchitis, sage for cleaning the blood and cough, rosemary to strengthen the heart, foxglove, which is digitalis to slow the pulse, borage and lambs-ear for wounds and arnica for sprains and bruises. I bet you could teach them all a thing or two, the doctor included. Remember, you have watched Granny and Bella your entire life!'

Most of the instructions seemed to be common sense and the rest she decided, she had to fake.

While the girls were busy studying the ledgers, Elsa and Angelika looked at each other:

"Should we tell them," started Angelika.

"Tell us what?" asked Maria.

"About the rats."

"What's special about rats? They're everywhere!" Maria was not impressed.

"Cook poisons them with arsenic."

"Well, that must have been it, because we saw a dead one and it had blood all around its muzzle."

"There you have it," said Elsa and shrugged her shoulders.

"Arsenic, I knew there had to be an easy answer."

Rose was not so sure. While they were discussing rats, she had moved onto the bed right next to Maria and Dora.

"I hate rats," she declared.

"Me too," said Dora, "if any of them have the nerve to come in here, I will kill them with my pocket knife, if I have to."

She pulled out a medium size army knife, flicking it open to expose a fairly large shiny blade. She slid it about ½ inch away from her neck across her own throat to prove her point. When the girls stared at her wide-eyed in disbelief, she started to laugh until she choked. Flicking the knife a second time, she flipped it back into its sheath.

"Seriously now, we saw a lot of them in the passageway. They were coming and going in an organized fashion, as if they had a purpose."

Now all eyes were focused on Angelika.

"Listen to the words of wisdom!" mocked Maria, who was still worried about being upstaged by this weird stranger. "Rats don't have a purpose, they are filthy rodents and we kill them. It's that simple. And that's the last I want to talk about this disgusting subject, end of story!"

Maria leaned back against the headboard of her bed and started to clean her fingernails with a slim wooden stick. That made Angelika look at her own ragged nails; she liked to chew when she was nervous.

Soon the rats were forgotten and the girls tidied themselves up to get ready for dinner. The dining hall was situated opposite the kitchen and was an imposing room. Dark walnut floors and panel-ing reaching halfway up the walls. A large table was standing in the middle with numerous chairs on either side. Matron was seated at the head and appeared to be waiting for everybody else to find their place. Two large candelabras in the middle of the table shone an eerie light all around accentuating the very dark shadows under Matron's eyes. She had placed her elbows on the table and rested her head on her hands while she was waiting for the chatting girls to sit down.

Angelika hung back. Elsa took the lead and momentarily every-one was seated and was paying attention. Angelika was trying to slide into one of the back chairs, hoping that they wouldn't even notice her, but Elsa pulled her right along with her and pushed her down into the chair next to Matron.

'Oh please God, help me, so I don't say anything inappropriate!' Angelika prayed.

When they were seated, Dr. James bounced in and greeted everyone again in his booming voice, thanking them for coming and reminding them that this was truly an important mission, and also reminding them that their reward will most likely be in heaven. As friendly and light-hearted as the speech appeared, it sounded ominous to the women, especially to Angelika.

"I hope our reward will not come too soon. I am definitely not ready for heaven," mumbled Maria.

Matron ignoring this remark, bent her head and said a little prayer in thanksgiving for the food they were about to receive. The door to the kitchen opened and two young girls appeared bearing large trays. They placed their burden in the middle of the table. Matron, Dr. James and the five girls had taken their seats around the top of the table. Angelika noticed quite a few empty chairs further down and whispered to Elsa, "I think they were expecting more help."

Elsa nodded. "I am sure we are only the first ones!"

'First ones, for what?' Angelika was getting more and more curious. Out loud she said, "Boy, I did not realize how hungry I was!" She had been too nervous and upset to pay attention to the grumblings of her stomach.

"I could eat a horse!" said Elsa, patting her extensive girth.

"I hope they don't shortchange us with food, we are already getting very little pay!"

Now Angelika wondered what in the world she could do with three hundred year old currency. Her stomach reminded her, that nothing mattered but the food. Apparently one can get hungry even in a dream! The platters were heaped with buttered bread and some kind of roasted meat, sliced into big slabs. It looked like ham or pork and there were bowls of stewed apples and turnips. They were not her favorite, but the brown bread looked crusty and the roasted meat tasted deliciously of smoke, as if it had been turned over a wood fire. Avoiding the turnips altogether, she took several helpings from the apples, which were scrumptious. While the girls were ravenously busy with their food, cook had brought in two pitchers of beer. Angelika never really liked beer, but she did not want to ask for anything else. After the first few sips, which were sour, but warmed her stomach pleasantly, she changed her mind. Maria who had watched Angelika carefully had noticed her hesitant approach to food and drink:

"I take it you are not used to ale. It's a bit stronger and a bit sweeter than regular beer. They brew it right here and it is often given to the patients. Sometimes we warm it for an extra effect on the blood pressure."

"Listen to our Maria!" said Dr. James. "She is absolutely right. There is often nothing better for reviving the feeble than a good strong draft of cook's warm ale!"

Angelika thought that he was spot on, since she was feeling a lot better after her second glass. Her new environment was losing its fear factor. By now she felt much more relaxed. There was pleasant warmth spreading throughout her limbs. Her head, which had a fuzzy feeling since she awoke in that rocking chair, now felt clearer, while her thought processes lost their nervous fright.

Cook, a small roly-poly body of a person, came in to accept her accolades from Matron, who praised her efforts, but then looking around at the girls, reminded them that this was their welcoming dinner and that from now on they will have to serve themselves, but only when time allows it, for the care of the patients comes first and foremost. She added that a common meal will be served occasionally when policies and procedures will have to be discussed.

While Angelika had eaten more from hunger than with appetite, she had noticed that Rose, who was seated on Elsa's other side, was only picking at her food. Right now she turned towards her and whispered, "How about the rats, we should ask cook, if she has poisoned them with arsenic?"

"Do you have anything to report, Rose?" Matron had taken her glasses off, rubbing her tired eyes; she focused her attention on Rose.

"I did not want to bring it up at dinner, but since we are all here, even cook..."

"Bring up what?"

"The rats! The awful rats and especially the dead one!" Rose looked down, her usual pink complexion had turned a few shades deeper, started to stutter. Elsa came to her aid:

"Matron, there seems to be a rat problem! When Angelika and I carried our water back from the pump, we saw quite a few in the passageway."

"I killed more than the usual amount that was sniffing around the flour bins," added cook.

"How did you do that?" asked Dr. James.

"The usual way, with that white powder out of those packets, we get mixed up by the apothecary. I have always used that, but this time it did not seem to work as well."

All this rat talk was getting too much for Matron. "This is really not the best dinner conversation. Let's finish so we can get on with our meeting."

Matron pushed away her plate and rang a bell. The girls from the kitchen appeared and started to clear the table.

"Leave us the ale, please," said Dr. James. "I think we can all use another glass!"

Matron waving a finger at the good doctor:

"Careful there, Jimmy, we will need a clear head! Now, for the reason you have all been summoned. There has been an outbreak, an epidemic of some kind in our little town. The old hospital and the field hospital on the other side of town are filled to capacity with the sick and unfortunately with the dying. People have been coming down with a strange illness."

At that point Dr. James got up and started to elaborate on the symptoms:

"The illness starts out like a common cold; with fever, swollen glands and lethargy. Some get better after a week, the swelling goes down, the fever breaks and the person recovers. Unfortunately most times the glands become very hard and bulbous. They are called buboes until they break open and the most ghastly puss oozes from them and, even then, some patients find relief and will recover, while for the less fortunate ones the fever rises, the person becomes delirious, is unable to take water and food and dies in great pain a few days later."

"We had a similar outbreak at our farm a few years ago," interjected Elsa, "my grandpa thought it was milk fever, but then it got worse, we had to kill nearly the entire herd and almost lost the farm. Fortunately once the sick animals were gone, the others recovered. We never really found out what the cause was. Grandpa thought it came out of the air and Grandma thought we had not prayed enough."

"Well prayers cannot hurt!" said Dr. James, looking at all the scared faces around him.

"For now we must be very careful; we shall isolate the sick ones, especially the ones with swollen glands which we shall lance and bandage. We have had some success with spirits and wine. Now that you know why you are here, you can still change your mind and we will send you home."

He glanced around at the five young women who looked frightened but also resolute.

Angelika thought, 'I wonder where I would go. What are the chances that I would wake up in Bella's hut?' She was just about to raise her arm, when she noticed Rose's fear-stricken little pale face and felt too guilty to go through with it. Besides, how would that clueless Dr. James get me home? It seems that I am condemned to stay with the others.'

She balled her left hand into a fist and reached under the table with her right for Rose's hand which was ice-cold.

Rose had not eaten a thing, just pushed her food from one side of the plate to the other, and broke down the meat into crumbles in an attempt to make it look less. Angelika whispered, "What's the matter? Don't you like anything on your plate?"

"I am just not hungry," Rose answered back in a shaky whisper.

Angelika was holding Rose's hand in hers to warm it, when the all familiar tingle assaulted her. She felt it first in her fingertips, then travelling up towards her elbow to become an almost painful sensation, like that of a mild electric shock, when one touches live current. Reflexively she pulled her hand back quickly and started to massage her arm, surprising Rose.

"Did I scratch you with my finger nail?" asked Rose.

"No, not at all, replied Angelika, I think my hand fell asleep or I got a cramp, that's all."

Meanwhile Dr. James had refilled their mugs with ale. Angelika grabbed hers and downed it in one giant gulp.

"Hey look at that one," laughed the good doctor, "she can be the house chugger!"

"Wait a minute! Here fill Rose's glass too. She is scared to death with all the talk about rats and the sick and dying people coming! We can use all the ale we can get."

Angelika never drank beer before, but she needed all the bravado it could provide her with to get over the shock of feeling the current in Rose's hand. She thought, 'This time I must be wrong, she is one of us and healthy.'

"Angelika, you seemed to be the brave one," Dr. James got up and came over to her chair.

"Why don't you come with me and show me that exsanguinated rat, which you girls have diagnosed." He took her by her elbow and gently pulled her off her seat.

"Cook will get us a bag and a shovel, so let's go and have a look- see."

This was truly the last thing Angelika was in the mood for; examining dead rats in 1679. 'If I could just wake up right now from this terrifying nightmare and go on with my real life. What was that by the way? Am I so far gone that I have forgotten my past?'

She gazed into Dr. James concerned and pleasant face, noticing his blazing blue eyes and thought: 'Well, at least he is cute; I could be stuck in my dream with Dr. Ugly!'

Cook brought the requested supplies and off they went in search of the dead rat. They lit the lamp, since it was already dark in the stairwell. Once they had descended into the passageway they encountered the grizzly scene. Unfortunately it looked at lot worse than before. This rat now had company! There were at least three totally dead rats and one smaller one in the throes of having a seizure, before it also collapsed and with a strange whistle, flopped over onto its side with bloody mucus dripping from its little rat fangs.

"Oh God, I am going to be sick!"

Angelika closed her eyes and tried with all her might to hold onto her stomach. She was telling herself: 'I am not weak; I am not vomiting in front of him, besides I don't want to waste all that good food and ale.'

While she was desperately trying to calm herself down, Dr. James shoveled the dead rodents into the bag, taking care not to touch them.

"I will take them to my laboratory, something is very wrong, and I have a good idea how this is related to this massive outbreak among our people. Take care not to touch anything. We have to get somebody to scour this place down. Meanwhile you girls make sure that you close your doors, put rags or blankets before any opening. I do believe that these creatures are contagious!"

"But how are they contagious?" asked Angelika, "Unless people get bitten or get in touch with their feces or perhaps their blood."

"Good thinking, but please take good care of yourself, I don't want to see anything happening to you, I like you!"

He had moved a little closer, almost invading her personal space, although she did not mind, she moved a step back out of habit. His eyes were full of concern and close enough that she could see that his blue irises were outlined with a darker blue ring. Or was it black? Too soon the mood was broken and the grizzly paper sack brought them back to reality.

"You don't have to worry about me," she laughed to bridge this slightly awkward moment, "I am made of tougher stuff. It's Rose, I am concerned about."

"The little red-head?" laughed Dr. James. "She might look like a pushover, but those red-heads surprise you every time. It seems like they don't feel pain like the rest of us. They bite down and push out a baby as easily as yanking out a tooth without much ado. It takes a lot to knock them out though. The only thing going against them is, they are known to be bleeders. One hates to generalize, but experience has taught us."

"Well, I am not a doctor, but she has no appetite, her hands were ice-cold while her brow was sweaty and she appeared quite shaken up."

"You may not be a doctor, but you may be better than that, a born healer," he joked, "for you observed all that, in a hand shake?"

'And so much more,' Angelika thought. 'But I am not telling, since I don't know you well enough'.

"Let's get back to the others, or they'll think we're up to no good!"

Dr. James put his arm lightly across her thin shoulders, which made her blush again, much to her chagrin. Silently she thought. 'No good, might be the ticket right now, it's better than dead rats!'

Angelika's experience with boys up to this point in time had not been too exciting and mostly benign. Some lame groping after a dance at the disco and a few harried kisses with one or the other of the eternally immature boys of her age had not amounted to anything worth discussing. So she had mostly listened when the subject came up, since she did not think she had anything exiting to contribute. Now Dr. James, he is definitely a candidate worthy of consideration. 'Let the nightmare get pleasant and exiting!' she thought with a last glance at the good Doctor and the rat bag he was carrying.

When they approached the dining hall, James put the oil lamp back on the table and announced to the waiting women, that he would be in his laboratory most of the night and wished for them to sleep well.

"How do we reach you, if we need you?" Angelika asked, still very concerned about Rose.

"All you have to do is ring for Matron; she will know how to get a hold of me!"

Angelika had noticed a quite extensive set of pulls and bells at the entrance of each hall way.

'No phone? What am I thinking?'

Again five pairs of eyeballs focused on her person. Instead of explanations which would have been useless, she just smiled.

At the table Matron was giving her last instructions for the following day when the patients were to arrive.

"We will meet here for a quick breakfast at 7 o'clock sharp! You girls have a good night sleep and I will see you in the morning."

With that the girls were released to their own devices. It was already after 8 PM and they decided to go for a quick stroll around the building, ending up at the terrible privy, before going to bed. They walked through the courtyard and Angelika braced herself for the parade of rats along the walls. She was relieved to see that the yard was empty. They were gone, vanished!

"I wonder where they have gone, there must have been a hundred!"

"I told you, that they come out at dusk and now they are feeding somewhere," said Elsa.

"Probably in our kitchen," muttered Dora in a flat voice.

"I think I will get my gun and shoot them the next time, they come out!" Elsa was full of bravado that none of the others felt.

"Guns and rats, what else?" Maria made a face and was shaking her head, looking at Rose:

"Come on Rose, let's get this over with!"

Poor Rose, still shaken and pale whispered, "Let's hurry outside for some air and then I want to lie down, I don't feel well at all!"

It was an early spring night; almost too balmy for the time of year.

"The weather is also very strange," said Maria.

Behind the hospital was a large garden with many trees, their branches still bare of leaves, showed the first beginnings of tiny buds and the tree trunks shimmered with an iridescent shade of green as if the juice of life reawakened by the sun was rising very closely to the surface of the bark.

"There are quite a few fruit trees here!" explained Elsa.

"This is an apple tree, that's a pear and that one over there is a cherry tree!"

"And how do you pretend to know that, since the branches are bare?" Maria had become exceedingly annoyed with Elsa's botanical lecture.

"That's easy! The tree always grows in the shape of its fruit! See, this here apple tree is round, shaped like an apple, and the pear tree is elongated much like a pear and cherry trees are much wider and have thinner branches than apple trees. And this one in the back is definitely a plum tree!"

Angelika felt so much safer with Elsa around than with any of the other girls. She was impressed by her knowledge, her steadfastness and general positive attitude.

"Always showing off!" Maria could not stand being upstaged, especially by a farm-girl.

"I bet you made this all up. If we are still here in the summer, those trees will prove that you are nothing but a liar!"

"Oh, come on, Maria, ease off!" Dora, the peace-maker, could not stand discord:

"I think there is some logic to what Elsa is proclaiming. But how about the plum tree; how can you possibly tell? Its shape is much like an apple tree and it's small and not wide or thin!"

"Again there is an easy answer," Elsa was not to be dissuaded.

"Plums do not ripen until very late in the summer, it has no buds, because it blooms last! Prune plums are the last fruit before winter apples!"

"Oh my God, what a show-off!" Maria was shaking her head in disbelief, "She just won't stop!"

They had all but forgotten about the rats, bantering happily back and forth, making their round through the garden, down the deserted cobble stone street around the hospital; their last stop being the privy, taking turns and waiting for each other.

"There is no light in the outhouse!" cried Angelika, which again brought on first stares of disbelief, then turning into raucous laughter from all four. 'Who ever heard of a light in the privy?'

A dim ray of pale moonlight shone through the crevices of the primitive wooden slats of the structure. She felt, more than saw, her way around the wooden seat. Lifting her heavy frock and apron with one hand trying not to touch the seat with any part of her anatomy, she desperately took aim for the middle of the hole without wetting her stockings and dress; the whole time hoping not to see rats or any other living or dead creatures. While the other girls found her discomfort curious, they waited good naturedly for her reappearance.

"Lordy, I hope you don't always take this much time; we are all gonna pee our pants!"

Elsa was laughing as she pictured all five girls with peed pants. Still chuckling, she grabbed Angelika's hand and together they ascended the steps back to the dormitory for the night.

Chapter 7
The Fine Citizens of Ratsberg

(It was the only way Angelika could think of the place!)

Just before they entered the building, Angelika turned around once more to take a look at the sleeping town. The streets were cobbled and quite narrow. Gabled red tiled roofs and half-timbered houses lined both sides of the street. The houses appeared even more ancient than the date she was given. She remembered seeing pictures of houses like this in her history books and her own medieval home town had preserved not only the original Altstadt (Old Town), dating from the 13th and 14th century, but a large piece of the original town wall from the same era built to protect the citizens from invasions of various tribes.

The beams were warped by weather and weight of the sandstone and horse-hair chinking. In many places the stone façade was cracking, exposing crumbling sand and straw. There were many small-paned windows, their frames as crooked as the house itself; leaning precariously to one side or the other, making strange configurations. Many of the house fronts looked like old and worried faces, lined up along the street, observing the good and the not so good inhabitants. Angelika especially noticed the window-glass. It was hand-blown, bubbled and flawed, it broke the light, slurring the view, much like someone's eyes would appear peeking out from behind coke bottle thick eyeglasses. One stray dog slunk along the open gutter and the humid early spring air could not dispel the odor.

'It is really strange,' mused Angelika, '1679 even smells different. It's a mixture of meat roasting, cabbage boiling and waste mingled with smoke and incense, not altogether unpleasant.'

By now the girls were getting used to Angelika's strange observations. Maria pulled her out of her reverie:

"As much as I would love to keep wandering about this dark and musty alley, it's time to get back home. The night is short enough already!"

"She is right," Elsa agreed, "we have to be at our best tomorrow!"

The whole time Rose was holding on to Dora's arm. She appeared quite weak.

"Let's go to our room! I think I need to lay down at once!"

Once they retired to their perspective beds, Angelika noticed, that the chest at the bottom of her bed was filled with undergarments as well as another dress and apron.

"Where did all this come from?"

She could not belief her eyes.

"It's my fault, said Elsa, "I told Matron that you needed a few things, since this assignment came as a total surprise to you!"

"Well, you have no idea!" Angelika was shaking her head. "I guess the magic does not stop!"

"If you call a few ugly dresses, drawers and wool stockings magic, be my guest." Maria laughed. "I am definitely used to finer things." She stroked her bodice and looked into her chest, where she had earlier piled her silky underpants and shirts decorated with hand-made lace.

"Well, we are all gonna get stinky and dirty in a short time, silk or linen, does not matter, it stinks the same. Silk is most likely worse for it is less absorbent. Flax and linen washes out better, is warmer and more durable. You have to be practical, girl!"

"Save it, farm girl! I for one like silk next to my skin, silk from Chinese silk-worms, spun beautifully just for me!" Holding one of her lacy nightgowns like a dancing partner, she was twirling grace-fully through the room.

"Oh, for God's sake!" countered Elsa, "I am surprised you did not bring your servants to help you with all your finery."

"I will do this myself, you just all keep your fingers off!"

"Don't worry; I would not want to be caught dead in scratchy lace and sticky silk; besides none of us would fit into your delicates, no doubt!"

"Please stop arguing!" pleaded Rose from her bed from the other side of the room, where Angelika was sitting beside her, checking her forehead for fever.

"My God, Rose, you are burning up!"

"Let's make a cool compress!" Elsa was immediately alerted, "Sorry, Rosie, I just get carried away sometimes."

They covered her with the extra blanket and watched her relax. Slowly her shivering stopped and she seemed to fall into a deep sleep. Elsa, Maria, Dora and Angelika looked at each other; afraid to utter a single word but they all thought the same thing!

Soon everybody had fallen into an exhausted sleep. Angelika could not get her mind off the rats. They had closed their door tightly and placed a few rags against the small slit between the door frame and the floor.

At one point Angelika thought that she had heard some rustling, but could not see any movement in the dim light.

It was still dark, when Matron knocked at the door. "Time to rise and shine!" she called kindly. "Get dressed and come down for breakfast, we need to plan our first day!"

They hurried into their clothes from yesterday. Angelika sniffed at her armpits, but could not detect any odor, except the furtive scent of lavender still clinging to her neck from Bella's hut.

Elsa was holding the oil lamp to shine their way to the dining hall, where cook had already laid out a simple breakfast of bread butter, jam and pitchers of milk.

"Well, at least we won't starve to death," Angelika was feeling a little hungry in spite of lasts night's rich fare. A pot of brown hot liquid stood in the middle of the table. Everyone poured a healthy serving into their mugs.

"This hot drink is the ticket to revive us," said Elsa cheerfully.

Angelika laced her mug with milk and sugar and took a big sip, which was a mistake, for she nearly spit it out, as soon as it touched her tongue. It did not taste like anything she had expected.

Matron looked at her:

"You will get used to our hot malt beverage. It is made from a grain. We grow it, roast it then grind it into a fine powder for this nourishing pick- me- up drink in the morning."

"I am sorry," Angelika blushed, feeling stupid. "I have never tasted anything like this before. Could I possibly have tea?"

"Tea is for the afternoon," grumbled cook, "but you can get your own, if you must."

Once they were seated, Matron pointed at the board in the front of the room.

"At 7 AM sharp, the first patients will arrive. I will be stationed at the door, deciding the severity of each case and direct them towards their stations. The sickest ones get placed as close as possible to our desk, for they will need constant attention and the lesser ones to their perspective beds down the line. The dying (here she took a break and wiped her tired eyes) will be taken into the back to the curtained-off area."

Angelika felt more scared than ever, she looked even paler than Rose, who after a good night's sleep seemed much recovered. She even reached for a second piece of bread, since she had not eaten much the night before.

Matron continued, "Elsa, I am putting you in charge of our intensive care area, where you will be assisted by Angelika."

'Oh thank you God,' thought Angelika.

"There will be about ten in your care. Maria, Dora and Rose will split up the others down the line. We will have room for thirty, but we can expand, if we have to. I will take care of the dying; perhaps Dora will give me a hand."

Matron had judged her little flock wisely; putting Elsa in charge of the sickest, where there was still hope and Dora with her excellent no nonsense approach to the back, where a somber mind and a solid constitution was of most importance.

Cook had set a special place for Dr. James, who was late. Most likely he spent the whole night staring at dead rats in his laboratory. Just then, he appeared, rubbing his red eyes and his hands to get some circulation back and hollered in good spirits:

"Give me one of your wake up specials my dear lady!"

Cook, who did never smile easily, blushed from ear to ear and hurried over with a plate and a steaming cup of that nasty brew.

"Lord have mercy!" laughed James, "One of these days, you will poison us all with this drink! I understand that there is a new drink on the horizon; derived from a little green bean that, if roasted, has quite a different aroma and affects the body like a stimulant. The Dutch are getting it from Africa and I have only tasted it once while

I was traveling. It was an exceptional experience, much more intense than the little rush one gets from a strong cup of black tea, if one can call that a rush!"

'He is talking about coffee', thought Angelika; 'they actually have never tasted coffee. This is really weird, but it all fits together. Coffee just had not made it to this part of the world.'

"You mean coffee," she blurted out.

"Well, listen to the world traveler here; you will make a great research assistant!"

Now it was Angelika's turn to blush. She quickly covered her mouth as not to divulge any more secrets.

"You will all be stimulated enough, when the patients are coming!" Matron used her knife like a gavel and order was once more restored.

"Cook will clean up, and everybody else will go to their stations!"

Elsa and Angelika checked out the first ten beds of the so-called ICU. Angelika had only ever taken a glimpse at an Intensive Care area before during one of her visits to the hospital when Granny was sick. At that time the constant ringing and beeping of alarms and the rushing about of doctors and nurses had intimidated her. This was altogether different; just beds pushed close together, no screens, no alarms, just one large desk in the middle from which all beds could be seen at all times. No electricity, no bells, no whistles, just beds, blankets and pillows, with each nightstand having its own supply of basins, large and small, beakers, strange looking bedpans with lids and stranger looking urinals. In the adjacent nurses' station were pots with salves, colored light creamy and black. Angelika was surprised by the brightly colored and strong smelling solutions in large beakers ranging from opaque to bright pink all covered with muslin rags and tied with string. There were glass syringes and metal needles, various red rubber hoses and clamps. Finely meshed linen cloth was cut to different size pads and there was one whole basket of the lightest, fluffiest gauze she had ever seen.

"I will show you how to make the best absorbing sponges from that," said Elsa, who had observed Angelika's curious explorations.

Behind the nurses' station was the medication room.

"We only keep a small supply of medicine here. Most of what we will need will come directly from Mr. Paulus the apothecary. He makes most of it to request for each patient. I will introduce you to him. He is a lot of fun and a fountain of knowledge. You will like the aroma there. On second thought, let's go visit him while we have a chance!"

They quickly walked along the corridor; down the steps, thankfully no rats made their appearance on their way to the famed apothecary. Angelika could already smell the herbs and see the steam pouring out from the small alcove in the basement.

"Mr. Paulus, are you there? I want to introduce you to our new friend Nurse Angelika!" This was the first time somebody had ever addressed her as such, which made Angelika swallow and take a deep breath.

"Come on in, my dear ladies!" called a cackling voice from the back. As their eyes had adjusted to the filmy steam they saw him; an ancient bent little man, white hair all the way down to his shoulders and sprouting from every orifice of his face. Two impressively bushy darker eyebrows shaded intelligent bright blue eyes, one of them protected by some type of single round glass, called a monocle which he was holding in his bony hand, while stretching himself to his full height as to examine these apparitions which had just materialized in his abode.

Angelika was momentarily shocked and too stunned to utter a single word. This Mr. Paulus could have been the exact male reproduction of Bella. The white wispy hair curled from the steam emanating from the great cauldron and the aroma of steeping herbs which pervaded the cavelike room, were such a strong reminder of her dear friend that her eyes filled with tears and she was too moved to trust her voice. When she finally whispered:

"It's caraway and fennel you are boiling? Right?"

"I am impressed, little one," said Mr. Paulus amused, "I gather you know your herbs!"

"Well, I had a good teacher," answered Angelika carefully.

"It helps. So did I, and, of course, all of my books." He swung his arms around to point out the many leather bound ledgers from famous doctors and alchemists; among them several editions from Paracelsus.

"Are you familiar with any of these?"

He had noticed Angelika checking out the many ledgers on his shelves.

"I know of Paracelsus, we learned about him in school, he coined the phrase: 'All things are poison, only the dose makes a poison not a poison.'"

"Bravo!" Mr. Paulus was clapping his hands.

"This is possibly the most important lesson of all. If we could just abide by that rule alone, how much unnecessary illness and treatment could be avoided!"

Elsa was getting impatient and was itching to leave. She was somewhat surprised again and taken aback by Angelika's strange knowledge. Thinking:

'This is one strange cookie, one minute dense as fog and in another she will blow your mind with facts we cannot fathom!'

"You girls better run, before they send out a search party, we will catch up later. I can hear carts; the sick will be on their way!"

With that Mr. Paulus turned his attention back to his steaming cauldron and his beakers.

They also heard some commotion and hurried upstairs, down the passageway, where to their chagrin; two rats seemed to be in the throes of a final seizure, before they flopped on their backs with bright red blood pouring from their muzzles. Too scared and disgusted to investigate this any further, they covered their mouths and noses with the masks they kept in their pockets and ran back to their station.

Mr. Paulus's hearing had not betrayed them. The sound of the creaking of carts being pulled and pushed was closer. As they approached the front gate, Angelika thought these carts looked like the handcarts she had seen being used on old farms. Two horse-drawn, cloth-covered wagons had also pulled up. Strangely garbed men, wearing long black oilcloth coats and similar head-coverings, gloves and masks started to unload their sad cargo onto litters to be brought into the hospital.

Matron had taken her position at the door and greeted each litter by assessing the prostrate body of its occupant. She did not believe in oilcloths and fancy masks. With confidence she felt their foreheads, counted their pulse and checked them for their general condition and alertness. Then she quickly reached underneath the blankets to check under the person's armpits and their groins, taking care not to expose them. The whole procedure took less than two minutes, enough for her to decide into which region of the hospital each person was being transported to. Angelika was impressed by her quick but gentle action and her sense of confidence and kindness with which she treated each individual.

The first three were sent towards the middle of the station. They were sick but awake and did not appear to be in too much pain. Two others were not arousable, but otherwise checked out to be in relatively good shape.

"Here these are yours, Angelika; let's put them up close, so we can keep an eye on them. They seem to be either comatose or sleeping very soundly."

Elsa helped her to get them situated in the first two beds. She made sure that they were placed on their sides with elevated heads to keep them breathing freely. The next three, a woman and two children seemed to be in more distress. Matron referred them to Dora. And so it went on for several hours.

Strangely clad men in black brought patients in various states of distress, while the girls settled them into beds, covering them with blankets and trying to keep them as comfortable as possible. Soon the ward was filled with about thirty patients. Angelika was impressed with how smoothly and relatively quietly the entire process unfolded, until one of the men asked Matron, what he should do with this last load.

"You mean there are more?"

Matron had asked Elsa for help and the two of them stepped out to look at the last cart. Meanwhile the men placed their strange looking oil-cloth masks over their noses and mouth once again. Angelika could detect an herbal essence emanating from the beaklike masks.

"What's in there?" she questioned one of them.

"Who knows?" was the short reply.

"Some kind of herbs to keep down the stench," said the other man. "It's no picnic Lady, when we have to get into their houses!"

Then Angelika heard Matron give the dreaded order:

"Please take these to the back, they are the worst ones yet, I will personally tend them!"

"Oh, Matron, let us help!"

Elsa and Angelika had overheard her commands and jumped in to help.

"Stop it, girls! This is not for you, these last three are in a terrible state; we will have to take extra precautions and we have to get Dr. James. I need you to go back to your station and worry about your lot."

A sad lot it was. Several hours had passed. They had undressed and washed each person and clad them into clean hospital shirts, which to Angelika looked much like the death-shrouds Granny and Bella used when they were summoned to take care of their dying friends.

"All clothes have to be burned!" was the last command Matron gave them before she and Dr. James went to the back of the station to tend to the dying there.

By now Elsa and Angelika had ten patients in their care; three girls, three boys, three women and one man. They had placed the women and the girls on one side together to give them more privacy, but none of their charges seemed to care. They were all feverish, red-faced with fleeting pulses and on the edge of consciousness.

"We need to cool them down, before they fry their brains," said Elsa. She placed basins with cool water on each of their nightstands and sponged them down about every half hour. She also wetted rags and wrapped them around their calves to prolong the cooling effect.

"We need to cool them, but don't get them to shiver, that will drive the fever up again," said Mr. Paulus, the pharmacist, who had brought up a white powder mixed in tea. Angelika was busy spooning it in between parched lips and hoping that the patients would be able to swallow it.

"One teaspoon every four hours, don't waste any, this is ground willow bark, great for fever, but I do not think there is enough of it in the world to cure this!"

He spread his arms wide, pointing at the bedraggled lot. After the second dose of the milky medicine, the once unconscious woman opened her eyes and started to look around. She was furiously search-ing for something or someone.

"Help, help!" she croaked. "Where are my children?"

Angelika had approached her and was holding her hand. "I think your girl is right next to you and your son is on the other side of the room."

"Are they dead?" was the woman's flat response.

"No, not at all, they are unconscious from fever as you were, and you woke up. I think they will be soon better, as well."

Angelika was trying to calm down the woman, who had raised herself on her elbows to get a glimpse of her children. She was wide-eyed and frantic.

"They are all dead, you know; my husband, my parents and the baby. We just laid down and waited for our turn."

"Well it looks like the men got to you in time. I think you will be better in a couple of days."

Angelika had held onto both of her hands in an attempt to keep the woman down and in bed. She had, up to this point, been way too busy to pay attention to any special feelings, that all too familiar current, she so dreaded. As she gently pushed the woman down, she noted that she felt nothing, no tingling and no sensation what-so-ever, just the strong pounding of the woman's pulse in her wrists. The woman was pale and sweaty and very thin, like she had not eaten in a long time, but Angelika knew with a strange certainty, that she would live.

"Elsa," she called, "please come and show me where Matron checks for swollen glands!"

Elsa, thinking that the woman was worse, stopped the sponging of the children and came to her aid.

"Glands are everywhere, but for this we check under the armpits and in both groins."

The woman's eyes were big and scared, when Elsa checked her with some pressure.

"Does it hurt, when I press here?"

"No, not at all, just my belly and my back but not there."

Elsa noticed the woman's extended belly.

"I will get Dr. James, but I think the worst is over for you. It's your liver that's swollen right now, that will take a while to get better. What's your name?"

"Marie," was the weak answer.

"Well, Marie, I think you will live!"

"How about my children? I don't want to live if they are doomed!"

"Listen to me, Marie! We will take good care of your children, all in good time!"

Elsa's confident and kind demeanor had calmed Marie to the point that she closed her eyes and drifted back into an exhausted sleep.

"I knew it, I knew it!" Angelika was happily dancing in-between the cots. "I knew she will live!"

"Stop it", laughed Elsa and then in a more serious tone:

"She may well be the only one."

That jerked Angelika back to reality.

"How about the children?"

"I really don't know, kids are different. They can look like death one minute and recover the next and vice versa. Now come over here, I want to show you what swollen glands look like."

Elsa had pulled her over to the male side, where she had started to bandage an old man's groin. The man's groin had exploded into the shape of a large apple or several apples. One had burst and the most hideous foul smelling green puss was oozing from the site. They had donned masks and gloves and special oil-cloth aprons, but the stench penetrated the thin gauze over their noses. Elsa pressed as much of the puss into a basin, while the man did not move a muscle or say a word. It seemed as if he was beyond this world. She spackled a large amount of strong smelling black salve over the wound until it was covered completely and rewrapped the bandage.

"This will have to be done at least three times a day, if we want to heal this."

Angelika was glad that breakfast had been hours ago and her stomach was totally empty, so nothing came up when she started to gag.

"Now you saw a bouboe," Elsa proclaimed. "It's a good thing it opened or James would have to lance it."

While she was redressing the man's wound, Angelika checked his forehead for fever and counted his pulse. Although he still seemed unconscious, his pulse was strong and his forehead not as hot as earlier. There also was no tingling, no current traveling up her arm.

"This man has terrible boils, or whatever they call it, that are breaking open, but I think he will live too."

"Is that your professional opinion?" Elsa joked.

"Yes ma'am that's it."

Angelika was moving happily from bedside to bedside, checking pulses, applying poultices, spooning medicine and changing sheets. When she approached a young girl's bed she stopped. Looking at the little emaciated body lying there red-faced and with labored breathing, she got scared. As Elsa taught her, she slipped her hand into the girl's armpits, and then pressed gently on her groins. Nothing out of the ordinary, she felt nothing.

"Oh, thank God, no glands!" she jubilated. "But she is so hot!"

"Children seem to run a higher fever than adults, that's quite normal," said Elsa, trying to calm her fears.

"This must be Marie's daughter!"

Angelika's hands lingered on the girl's body, but again there was no sensation, no tingling, just heat, terrible heat.

"What else can we do, to cool her down?"

"Nothing else than what we are doing already."

Elsa's broad hand was gently swabbing the child's dry mouth and cracked lips.

"Our old country doctor, the one that took care of us and the animals was always of the opinion, that a body can heal itself from just about anything and that fever is part of that healing. This guy believed in some kind of invasion of the body by tiny animals, too small to see. He believed that a good fever burns up these invaders. And we do see it all the time; the fever breaks, the body sweats, out come all the invaders and the person gets better."

"He seemed to be a very wise one, your people and animal doctor," replied Angelika.

"By the way, I could eat a horse, speaking of animals." Elsa was patting her expansive girth, laughing. "I did not get this by starvation."

Even Angelika felt her stomach growling; green puss forgotten, she was also looking forward to dinner.

"No wonder we are starving, we've missed lunch! If this continues, we will miss quite a few meals!"

Elsa now looked more worried than when she was bandaging oozing buboes. The idea that, in Elsa's eyes, missing meals was the scarier of the two, made Angelika laugh out loud.

Elsa had Dr. James check on the children, since she felt that the little boy was not responding to the fever medicine, she had tried to spoon in between his clenched lips. Angelika, who had observed her efforts, was equally concerned about this boy. He was bright red and his little chest was heaving with the effort to breathe, and his little face was drawn into a grimace as if he were in a great deal of pain. Elsa had pulled all of his clothes off and continued sponging him with tepid water until James was able to see him. Suddenly the doctor's demeanor changed.

"Help me turn this little fellow on his side, so I can listen to his lungs!" he asked Angelika. He then placed a clean linen cloth directly over the child's back and pressed his ear against it. 'Wait,' Angelika thought, 'no stethoscope?'

"No stethoscope?" She blurted out.

"What did you just say?" James looked at her with concern.

"Did you just say stethoscope? That's Greek for chest and scope means to examine. You are a very strange girl," he mumbled.

"If you say so, Dr., I don't know any Greek!" She tried to hide her amazement at this utterly primitive approach. But it was only 1679 and the stethoscope would not be invented for another 150 years. 'I better shut up or they will put me into a loony-bin', she thought. As she was holding this little boy's fever wrecked body in her hands, she felt the familiar tingling of electric current shooting up her arm. It was so powerful, that it made her whimper:

"I think, it looks really bad for this little one."

They checked his arms and legs and found plenty of swollen glands and a distended belly.

"You are right, my dear, this one is not long for the world, but you never know, children can surprise you."

"Not this one," was her sad reply.

"And you know that? How?" He looked at her with some surprise.

Angelika just shrugged her shoulders, "Well, I just know, please don't ask me how, I don't really know, but I am too often right!"

They then made the boy as comfortable as possible, giving him a few drops of Mr. Paulus's pain-mixture, which was opium, arnica and willow bark.

It had gotten late and Matron directed half of her nurses and the good doctor to wash up and take a break in the dining hall. Elsa and Dora stayed behind to be relieved later. It was a tired crew, Maria, Rose, Angelika, Matron and a few volunteers from town, who now gathered around the table. There were baskets of freshly baked bread and a cauldron of soup placed in the middle. Angelika noticed that Rose in particular looked about as poorly as she did the night before. While she herself felt bone-tired, she was not without appetite. Rose just looked at the food and said in quiet voice:

"May I be excused please? I think I will lay down first and have a bite later!"

Angelika took her arm and guided her through the passageway up the steps to the dormitory. Rose was deathly pale and half way up the steps, she leaned most of her weight on Angelika. Once upstairs, she got undressed and laid down. Almost immediately she started to shiver uncontrollably.

"I am getting James for you, no excuses!"

Angelika ran downstairs taking several steps at once. The good doctor had just piled thick slices of that delicious bread on a plate next to his stew, when Angelika approached him breathlessly:

"Rose is sick; you must see her right away!"

"Hold your horses! First we will eat, you too, my dear, if we want to stay alive through this!"

Angelika's stomach was grumbling painfully at this point and when cook handed her a tray loaded with steaming stew and bread, she threw herself into it, heart and soul and for a moment almost forgot about Rose. One of the helpers came in with large pitchers of dark ale and before she could wave them away and ask for water, James had filled two large tankards and offered one to her. He said with a twinkle in his eyes:

"Mud in your eyes!" and then took a large draught.

Angelika had not realized how hungry and thirsty she had been. After the stew was gone and most of the ale drained, she looked up and around, meeting Maria's amused eyes:

"Well, well, look at our fine young city girl; she certainly has an appetite and thirst like any old field-hand I have ever seen!"

Angelika almost apologized for her greed and poor manners, when James intervened:

"Girls, you have to eat a lot and sleep as much as you can, so your healthy constitutions can take over and get you through!"

Matron nodded; "Listen to him; this is apparently very contagious and we have to protect ourselves, so we can be of use. All we can do is, stay strong and be clean. After that it's up to God!"

After the stew, cook surprised everybody with a big apple cobbler, stewed apples, raisins and lots of ginger and cinnamon butter.

"Mm", said Angelika, "I have not tasted anything this good since Bella's hut."

"Who is Bella and where is her hut?" asked Matron. While all eyes were focused on Angelika, she felt compelled for the first time to tell them a little about Bella and Granny, being careful to keep the story in 1679. Apparently they did not think it unusual for an old witchy woman to live in a hut at the edge of the forest and many had an old wise granny. So they listened, nodding their heads in agreement and thought her story quite plausible, which it was.

Then they remembered Rose. Cook had fixed a tray for her, which Angelika was to take up to the room and Dr. James fetched his bag with medicine. Maria stayed in her seat; taking it all in, glowering at Angelika, who acted as if she did not notice. It was slightly passed twilight and as they went through the hall and up the steps, the passageway was teaming with rats, one curious parade coming along one side of the wall and one going along the other side. They stayed out of their way in the middle, Angelika right behind James.

"That's what you meant, by an organized fashion," acknowledged James.

"This is really quite gruesome, we have to do something, there is a connection between these rats and this out-break, I know it. I wish that I could prove it!"

"At least they're not dead, I never thought in all my life I would be happy to see live rats," cried Angelika.

The ale had done its job. Her head was spinning slightly and some of her apprehension had disappeared.

"Cook needs to put out more poison or better poison. I must speak to Paulus!" James was trying to be reassuring.

Once they entered the room, they closed the door tightly and placed the rags back under the door. Angelika put her tray on the table and the good doctor sat next to Rose on the bed. They realized immediately that she was in a bad way. She was bright red, her body was burning up and when Angelika felt under her armpits, she found her glands swollen and hard under her fingertips.

"Oh no, James, Rose has it!" She cried and tears filled her eyes. They looked at each other in disbelief.

"We need to isolate her; you will stay with her, while I get Matron to make the arrangements. God damn it!" He was mad and frightened at the same time.

"She had it last night," whispered Angelika. "She probably had it when she came. I knew it at dinner time, when I felt her hand, she had no appetite then. Will she die?"

"I don't know, you seemed to be the expert in that department!" Rose was nearly unconscious; turning her head from side to side, she murmured about her mother and brothers, but neither Angelika nor James could make any sense of it.

"Matron will send somebody to alert her family."

As they left Rose's bedside, James took both of Angelika's hands, looking into her eyes, he declared in a very serious voice:

"We need to take precautions now. For one thing, we will not disclose any of this; it will stay between us and Matron. There is no use frightening the others. I believe that she came to us already infected. It has hardly been two days. We will wash carefully. I don't know exactly why, but those who keep very clean, seemed to get infected less. It makes no sense since they say that it comes from the air. Now if she does not get the pneumonic type, just the swollen glands we can lance, she might have a chance. If she starts coughing blood, it will be over in three days."

James looked very serious and sad and while Angelika was trying to take this all in, he continued:

"I studied the ancient ledgers for most of last night; we can try using some of the concoctions mentioned there; plasters made from mustard and onions and pastes of garlic and sage can be applied to open wounds. Also the washing with vinegar and old wine seemed to help in some cases."

"I just hate it when you have to lance these glands; the scream- ing is really hard to tolerate."

"That's true, but the relief that comes with extracting that vile puss is worth it." They took one more look at Rose. He felt her fore- head and counted her pulse. With a last look and feel at her swollen glands, he mumbled:

"Not ready yet, but perhaps by tomorrow!"

Angelika stayed with Rose, while James heaved himself up off the bed and left the room in search of Matron. She was anxiously watching her labored breathing, fearing the worst and wondering what type of precautions they could possibly take. After counting her pulse again, which was rapid and weak and while she was holding her wrist she knew with certainty that no amount of washing with wine, applying poultices and lancing could save Rose. She felt little electric shocks travelling up her arms and no matter how she was trying to deny that sensation, it was there. Rose was doomed. Angelika knew it yesterday at dinner while everyone else held hands for the prayers Matron insisted on before meals.

By now Rose's temperature had risen to dangerous heights, her body was burning up and her swollen glands were straining against the taught skin of her groins and armpits. Angelika was trying to alleviate her suffering by sponging her body with diluted tepid wine. Rose mumbled unidentifiable words in her feverish state, throwing her body restlessly from side to side and feebly reaching for unseen objects in the air, when she was not picking at her bedclothes. Angelika had observed this type of behavior before when she had snuck into the single room for the dying, while visiting Granny in the hospital.

Suddenly Rose opened her eyes and with glassy bright green irises focused her attention unwaveringly onto Angelika, who had bent her head close to Rose's face in an attempt to understand her murmuring. With a raspy voice, that was surprisingly strong Rose asked:

"Where do you come from? You must be a witch, because you knew, you knew......" At that her weak but venomous voice trailed off and she resumed her feverish mumbling and picking.

'She thinks that I am a witch! After all, this only 1679. Perhaps they all think I am a witch, because I am odd and I seem to know things.' thought Angelika. She was furiously trying to remember the few historical facts about witch-hunting from her history classes. It seemed so long ago since she had had a normal life, school, friends, Bella. If it weren't for that blasted tea in Bella's hut! It seemed like a lifetime ago, yet it had only been two days since she awoke to this living nightmare. Again she took in her surroundings and after pinching her cheeks vigorously, she had to admit to herself that this was the reality dealt to her and not a dream.

Her thoughts were racing; 'when did they burn witches? Was it earlier or later? It had to have been centuries ago, during the 'Middle Ages' not during this time of Restoration.'

She remembered the old walled city of her upbringing. There were witches towers at all corners still intact and the butt of their jokes and threats they played on each other. Those towers stemmed from an earlier time; she remembered clearly the old writing on some of the houses which dated as far back as the 12th century. Most citizens by now must have gotten over their superstitions. But then, wait, how about America? There were witch hunts and burnings in Salem Massachusetts. That had to have been much later, as late as the 18th century. But then America was probably behind the times.

Stroking Rose's burning and blotched face, which seemed to get smaller by the minute, the hot taut skin pulled tightly around her delicate bone structure, Angelika said out loud:

"Rosie, my dear friend, I am not a witch, I just have feelings and certain sensations I have had all my life. Often they tell me about a person's health, but just as often I am dead wrong!"

She regretted her choice of words and the fact that she was lying. Rose's sunken eyes popped open again, her mouth twisted into an ugly grimace and she hissed over and over:

"Witch, witch, cause of all evil!"

'My God,' Angelika thought, 'they might think that I caused this disease, this plague or whatever it is.' This was actually too frightening to consider, so she decided that it was absolutely necessary for her to hide her gift or her curse from everyone.

Matron and Dr. James had entered the room. While Matron appeared quite upset that Angelika was not wearing her protective mask and apron while she was tending Rose, she clearly took command of the situation.

Two orderlies with a litter entered the room and Rose was lifted of her sweaty sheets and carried downstairs.

"Please take her to the back of the ward, where I will personally take care of her!" Once the orderlies returned; according to Matron's instructions, they scrubbed the bed, added new sheets and removed all of Roses belongings.

"Normally we would open all windows, but I don't think that's best right now, so we will burn a lot of sage to purify the air."

She produced a fairly large bronze vessel which was filled with beeswax. As the pale green sage was starting to smolder, an eerie light illuminated their anxious faces and bathed the room with a calming scent.

Dr. James looked absolutely stricken, his sad face and demeanor told Angelika that most likely she was absolutely spot on with her diagnosis.

'How to hide my knowledge?' she mused. 'It may well get me killed, if the others think like Rose.'

Not Dr. James. He was under the impression that what upset Angelika was the fact that Rose had gotten sicker during his absence. He tried to comfort her, as she was fighting back tears.

"Please come to my office as soon as possible. We have to talk!"

Angelika gave Matron a shy look, but Matron replied:

"You go ahead dear, for there is nothing you can do for Rose at this time. Go with James and have him pour you a stiff drink, you look like you need one and when you're done bring me one as well!"

'Thank God she has a sense of humor; it looks like we will need it.'

All three of them stared at the empty space where Rose's bed had been and they all had the same thought:

'Will there be more and how soon?'

As soon as they left the room, James put a protective arm around Angelika leading her down the steps where several rats hurried away from their approach and their voices along the dark corridor to James's study. He closed the door behind them and led her to an old overstuffed easy-chair, mumbling:

"Got to keep those blasted rats out. I am convinced they have a direct connection to this outbreak! Everywhere in my old medical ledgers is talk about the occurrences of dead rodents, birds even cats and dogs whose bodies were crawling with lice."

Angelika shuddered at the thought. By now she looked even paler and more distraught than before.

"How about that drink," she ventured, thinking; 'I have drunk more alcohol in these last two days, than any time during my life before. Perhaps this is truly a nightmare and I am just dreaming up all this liquor.'

James poured a healthy measure out of a big brown bottle into two tumblers, splashing a little water onto the strong drink before handing one to Angelika.

"What is it?"

"Arrak," was the short answer. "It's a type of rum drink the sailors swear by when accosted by disease."

"Did you get that from your old ledgers as well?"

"No, not really, I knew it already. I have tried this antidote plenty of times myself, and it has always served me well! See, healthy as a horse and planning to stay that way!"

With that he started to jump up and down, beating his broad chest and smiling from ear to ear. He gave Angelika her drink and brushed against her hand in the process. Angelika felt a jolt, not a tingle at all but a different sensation, one that she had never experienced before. It was a jolt combined with pleasant warmth that spread from her arms to the middle of her stomach, her solar plexus contracted and the pleasant tingling worked its way down across her belly, making her tighten her abdominal muscles and then down towards her thighs. While the tingling and warmth traveled across her lower body, a steady throb concentrated around her pelvis, creating a sensation similar to the one she had felt before when kissing and petting with her school boyfriend. Similar, but not exactly the same.

This was stronger, more demanding causing an ache which was pleasant a first, but then turned to heat, which her body relieved by pouring it out. Holding her drink in shaking hands and attempting a first sip from this antidote, she desperately tried to hide her feelings from the man. Concentrating on swallowing the fiery brew and her poker face, she joked:

"I can see, how your mind works, trying to get me drunk, so you can have your way with me, Dr. James. I like to know, how many lovely girls have been in this easy chair, holding a strong drink?"

It was meant to be a joke, but it came out all wrong, prudish and simple. He took the drink from her shaky hands.

"I hope you do not think me a thoughtless Lothario, leading unsuspecting maidens into my lair. I just want to keep you alive in this hell, for you are truly a special sort of girl, the likes of which, I have never met before."

'You have no idea how special', she thought. 'I am not even from your century, a figment of your and for all I know my own imagination. But why do I feel such an attraction, why do I feel drawn to him? It's as if I have known him always, not like those other boys. Nothing I have experienced before compares.' This time she took a big sip, feeling the strong liquor burning all the way down her throat to her gut.

"Angelika," he said in a hoarse voice, "I really care about you and I don't know exactly why."

He had gotten down on one knee to be on eyelevel with her, gently removing the glass from her hands, he placed them into his warm ones, turning her palms up, he bent his head and kissed them.

'No, please God, no, not the palms!'

Just for a split second he rested his cheeks in her open palms and murmured softly:

"For everything you do."

Before she could react to this turn of events, he jumped up, tossing the rest of the Arrak back, looking at her shocked expression, he said dryly:

"And now it's time to do more; the patients are waiting. Let's dazzle them with our knowledge and your intuition!"

'Boy,' she thought. 'He certainly can turn the charms on and off at a whim. I need to be careful and learn how to handle this, whatever this is.'

Still puzzled by the powerful sensations his touch had aroused in her, she gathered her wits about her, trying to forget the sweetness and the resulting moisture between her legs, she got up as well. Steadying her slightly dizzy head, they walked together down the passageway back to the ward, which by now was filled with the sick and the dying.

"We forgot Matron's drink!"

"No fear, Jimmy is here," he laughed and patted his bulging coat.

"I brought it with us."

Every bed was filled. Outside the death carts were rattling by. Every couple of minutes one of the porters, covered in slick black oil-covered cotton coats and similar masks stuck their head in the door enquiring about the possibility of an empty bed in the ward, hoping that some would die quicker as to relieve them of their load.

"Bodies are piling up!" somebody yelled.

"Up to a thousand so far! The cemetery is full; gravediggers are working overtime, no more coffins to be had!"

This terrible litany did not stop. Finally Matron put an end to this, before shutting the doors firmly, she shouted:

"Out with all of you, this is still a hospital; we do the best we can!"

"Well, in that case, we will just leave them on your doorstep," said the black clad man.

"You will do no such thing, treat them as human beings and care for them with respect, you will!"

Matron was outraged by the man's callousness, until she stepped outside and winced at the misery piled on one of the carts. Quickly she waved the orderlies over to carry as many as they could and place them on pallets on the floor between the bedsteads of the sick. It was difficult to get between the pallets and the beds. Elsa was in full swing. She and Dora worked tirelessly hand in hand. It was, as if, they were thriving on this adversity. Only Maria continued to carry her nose up high, like she was trying to escape that pervasive smell of death and decay, but ultimately she set her jaw and dug in. Angelika was full of admiration for all of them. Too tired to think independently, she followed orders, did as she was told and prayed for guidance.

Chapter 8

The Agony and the Ecstasy

Death carts kept rolling past the hospital. They hardly stopped anymore. There was little hope for those unfortunate souls in these rolling bins. Once a person fell ill, the entire household, including the unaffected, was locked up, closed to the outside world. They called it 'Quarantine'. What it meant in reality was that everybody inside was now doomed. If they did not die of plague, they soon perished from starvation. This was the reason why many of the sick early on were hidden; no doctor was summoned for fear of isolation and the 'Quarantine'. Often the ones who were still well would sneak out late at night foraging for food. Even the garbage dumps were searched. One had to be quick to beat the roaming rats to the goods. Rats have a ferocious appetite. Once the garbage dumps and bins were empty, there were plenty of corpses to feast on. Curiously not all rats fell ill either. James had examined many of their corpses, especially the ones Cook had poisoned and found this very perplexing. It seemed as if some gained strength by possessing some type of immunity against this miasma, much like some people.

A meeting with the mayor had been called for the leaders of the small town; the business owners, the pharmacist and the few doctors remaining, since most others had fled the city with the first sign of the outbreak. Preventive measures were discussed at length. Most of the doctors took to wearing slick black oiled long coats with the beak-like black leather helmets. They hoped that the crushed incense and herb packages stuffed into the length of the beak would protect them not only from the abominable stink but from the disease itself.

During their meeting they admitted that they did not touch their patients anymore. They used long sticks which they pointed at the affected body parts, while the relatives of the fallen were asked to turn the sick person. Dr. James found this altogether distasteful:

"How can one possibly examine someone without touching them? They are acting like we are still in the dark ages, when sticks were used to examine women, because it was deemed improper to touch another man's wife."

Shaking his head and pounding his fists, he continued:

"I, for one, will not wear that coat and that ridiculous helmet. If you are meant to catch it, you will, no matter how much incense you burn."

"So you believe in the curse then, the one that's sent down from heaven as punishment from the almighty!" an old doctor with a long beard and twinkly eyes, leaning heavily on his gnarled cane, asked. He was puffing a huge pipe full of aromatic tobacco, creating a foggy shield around his person.

"I don't believe in incense, curses and prayers for all that matters. I do believe that those rats are the culprit. I believe that this disease is carried from them to us, perhaps through their fleas and lice."

"Be very careful, my friend!" The old smoking fellow raised his voice, "be careful not to anger the priests and the bishop with your speculative science. It could be easily misunderstood and you could be jailed as a heretic, no matter how sound your observations are."

"So you think they're sound?"

James could barely hide his excitement. He had always liked the old experienced doctor, the only one in their small group who also did not wear a coat and a helmet. He trusted him and valued his judgment.

"You must let it go, do the best you can and try to stay alive. I am old, my life is almost over, but I will help you as much as I can," was his well-meant advice to his young colleague.

"Order!" the mayor shouted, "What are we going to do about the dead"?

They decided upon the opening of mass graves, since the coffin makers were running out of available lumber. It had only been two days since the opening of the hospital and the number of dead exceeded the number of the sick and dying. As soon as a bed was freed, the body removed as quickly as possible, the bedstead scrubbed and fresh sheets applied, a new poor soul became its next occupant.

Matron now had the grim task of selection; giving the bed only to those who faired a chance of recovery. Those who laid in extremity were given some opiates to relieve the pain, but no real hope. Several sisters from the local nunnery came to help and to relieve the girls at night.

Since Dr. James was convinced that people contracted this infection by either contamination from rats or from each other, he insisted on fierce hand washing and changing of clothing immediately after the girls left the patients. The girls scrubbed themselves from head to toe with vinegar water and changed into clean dresses and shoes, a practice unheard of. Even Matron thought that he was going overboard with his crazy cleanliness. He also insisted on having all worn articles boiled with lye soap and ironed with a hot iron after drying in the sun.

"Jimmy," she worried, "with all this extra work in the laundry, I am going to have to sweet talk my ladies down there, so they won't quit on us!"

"And where, do you think they are going to? It's hell out there. They are lucky to have a clean place to work and sleep," he responded dryly.

Angelika was ever so glad to escape the stench and cries for a little while. They gathered in the dining hall this evening of the second day, where cook had laid out a cold supper of sliced roast beef, boiled eggs, good strong yellow cheese, and dark rye bread. The crowning glory in the middle of the table was the pitcher of strong ale.

"Is everybody well?" asked matron.

"Let's say a prayer and then let's eat. We need to keep up our strength. If we weaken, we cannot do anything for anybody." She picked up the pitcher und poured big mugs for everyone.

"I don't know about you, but I am parched, first we drink then we eat!"

Angelika marveled at the group of women who had shown such strength and fortitude in the face of horror, especially Elsa and Dora.

"Should we not first check on Rose?" Angelika knew that Rose had been on everyone's mind.

"Don't mind her; she is in good hands, while we are resting! Her fever has not risen any higher, her buboes have been lanced and now she is in God's hands. It's the best we can do!" With that said Matron took a big gulp from her mug and urged the girls to do likewise.

Knowing what God had in mind for Rose; Angelika picked up her mug with shaking hands and took a deep draught which almost made her choke.

"That a girl," laughed Elsa reaching for a large chunk of bread and a slab of meat.

It had been unseasonably hot, which seemed to be spreading the disease at a more rapid pace. It was as if the hot moist air was forcing germs into every crevice. Even breathing was more difficult. One had the sensation that the damp heat was trying to suffocate all that was healthy and clean. The town and its inhabitants laid captive within a steamy unhealthy miasma of death where there was no escape.

Thankfully the dark paneled walls of the dining hall were thick enough to keep the worst of the heat outside, giving the illusion of cool order and reprieve. After the second mug of ale, Angelika felt the now familiar lightness and finally the first hunger pains which made her greedily reach for bread and cheese.

"I don't understand how you all can eat at a time like this?"

Maria had sat quietly observing the group with her natural disdain.

"Rose is dying and you folks eat and drink as if you are at a party. I just wonder who will be next."

"Listen up!" Elsa snorted between bites of meat and sips of ale.

"Whether we eat or not eat will absolutely make no difference in Rose's condition. We must keep our strength, if we are to return to our posts tomorrow morning. I prefer to be doing it with a full stomach and a rested body."

"She is right," Matron interrupted their conversation, "we mean no disrespect to Rose. We need to keep ourselves going, if we are going to be of use!"

"She can't leave either," said Dora, "she has to be in Quarantine for some weeks before she can return home."

'I guess that does not exactly apply to me,' thought Angelika, 'Why can I not simply wake up in that rocking chair in Bella's hut and call this a nightmare?'

Out loud she said, "Oh Maria, let's just eat and then we will go to check on Rose before we go to bed."

"You will do no such thing!"

Dr. James had entered the dining hall and overheard Angelika's last remark.

"Remember you are all cleaned up, so your visit will have to wait until morning."

"If she is still with us," Angelika mumbled under her breath. Greedily she poured another measure of ale into her cup and took a deep draught to dull the pain and anguish she felt.

Meanwhile the conversation at the table had turned to lighter topics and somebody even tried to tell a joke or two. The effect of the beer helped to ease their minds and lessened the body pain they were all experiencing from the constant effort of turning and lifting the sick. The platters were getting empty and the pitchers were down to the dregs, when cook burst on the surface, announcing that supper was now over. She still had to clean up and she dreaded having to make her way through the crowded streets in the dark.

"Why don't you just stay with us?" asked Matron. "Is there anybody at home that needs taken care of?"

"No Ma-am, there is nobody, my husband died years ago and we never had little ones. These girls here have been my charges," cook said pointing at Elsa and Dora. With that said she grasped the furthest corner of her white apron, covering her impressive girth, and wiped a few escaping tears from the corners of her eyes.

"Well then it's settled. You will stay in the servant's quarter; there is plenty of room there, since most of the other housekeepers have left since this curse started."

"I'll be much obliged Ma'am, you are very kind, and the streets are not safe anymore," she continued wiping at her eyes and was obviously moved by their generosity.

"It's all right, dearest cook," Elsa had jumped up and gave her big bear hug, "you have always been one of us."

The girls got up, carrying their empty plates and mugs back to the scullery. They decided to take a short walk through the courtyard before retiring to their dorm room. Matron had posted guards in the front and back of the property to keep out the most desperate.

"If we don't protect ourselves, we cannot help the sick and needy," was her constant mantra.

Before they left the dining hall, James had called to Angelika to meet him in his study. He wanted to show her the results of his last research.

"I can only imagine what it is he wants to show her," Maria hissed venomously under her breath.

James had overheard her remark and added:

"You may come along, dear Maria if you are interested. This is not a secret."

"That's all right!" she countered, holding her pretty head up high.

"You can surprise me along with everyone else once you have found a cure!" With a haughty sneer she turned around saying:

"Come on, girls, let's get a breath of air, it's awfully stuffy in here!"

James took Angelika's hand, not listening to her excuses; he dragged her along the passageway towards his study.

"Now you have done it; she hated me before and now it's over. I better watch my back. That Maria sounds downright vicious."

"Oh, she is all bark and no bite."

James was quite amused at this display and appeared flattered by their rivalry.

"How long have you known her?" Angelika was getting suspicious at this point, thinking: 'If he had a fling with her, I am definitely out of here.'

"I have known her exactly as long as I have known you, but first impressions hardly ever lie."

"So what's so important, that you have to share it with me tonight?"

"It's the fact that I have discovered two different types of rats. Cook killed them all with the same poison. The sick ones were smaller

and they seemed to be crawling with fleas, whereas the bigger health-
ier rats showed no signs of the bleeding disease and had fewer or no
fleas at all. It appears that the fleas were drawn to the smaller sickly
species. I believe that the fleas are directly responsible for this outbreak. I have studied the old ledgers and found many articles which
make a direct connection to the spreading of this disease through filth
and dirt which comes with poverty and exposure. For instance in the
Jewish ghettos, even though many were poor, the healthy and clean
living conditions preached to the believers in the Talmud, seemed to
have protected them."

"Yes, but were they not also a closed community with fewer
connections to the outside world?" Angelika was trying to understand what she was hearing.

"That is true to a point, but most Jews were salesmen, vendors
who bought and sold their goods outside the Ghetto during the day.
Only at night were the gates closed and guarded, just like they are
now. It must be cleanliness, bathing rituals and the strict separation
of meat and dairy. Perhaps even the way the animals are kept, fed and
slaughtered. Look here!"

He pulled down a huge ledger written in an ancient script.

"What kind of hieroglyphs are those?"

"Well it does not go back quite that far. It is Arabic and here it
is translated into Hebrew. Look at these pictures."

Angelika could hardly believe her eyes. It was an ancient copper
engraving depicting a Jewish village burning. People were running
for their lives, others were flinging burning torches onto the closely
nestled roofs of their houses. People themselves were on fire, running
torches, while the slaughtered animals littered the road with their
twisted carcasses.

"It says under here, during an outbreak of the pocks in the 12th
century this Jewish Ghetto was inexplicably spared. For that reason
alone the good Christians, the papists, decided that the outbreak had
to be brought on by the nonbelievers, since they did not die at the
same rate as the Christians. No other explanation was needed, problem solved. Thank God we do not live in the dark ages anymore."
James concluded.

"We don't?" Angelika swallowed hard and nearly gave her secret away. She added carefully: "I think you are on the right track. There are germs, little living things we cannot see, which can make us sick. Just because we cannot see them, does not mean, they don't exist."

'Oh God, can I tell him about bacteria's and viruses as little as I know about these things. It could shed a light on all this laborious research he is doing. Most likely he will laugh and think that I have a great imagination. But I cannot take a chance; Rose already thinks I am a witch.'

"You are absolutely brilliant, my dear girl." Dr. James grabbed her hand, pulling her out of her reverie, and then started to twirl her around the room until she felt quite dizzy. Once he steered her into an easy chair he said:

"Let's drink to this, wait; you are over eighteen, right?"

"Eighteen on my last birthday," she replied dryly, eying up the big brown bottle with the strong smelling potion which momentarily was being splashed into two waiting tumblers of rough cut glass.

"Remember the antidote; I keep it in my bureau."

"Quite well, first it burns like hell and then it warms me all the way to my toes."

"That is exactly what it is supposed to do my dear." He pulled a small chair in front of her comfy one and handed her the glass.

"Down the hatch, Cheers!" Angelika took only a little sip since she was already slightly headachy from the earlier ale and was afraid that the extra alcohol might seriously loosen her tongue. She took another sip and then resolutely put her cup down. Straightening up to her full height she declared in no uncertain tone:

"Well, my dear doctor, if your intentions are to be getting me drunk and then have your way with me, I must disappoint you. I am not that kind of girl, even in the face of death; for we do not know what will happen to us. I have read the historic ledgers and although I have never been good at math I believe that most of us are going to perish, before this is over."

James had listened to her fairly long speech. He put down his empty glass, looking intently into her worried face and eyes brimming with tears, he gently reached for her trembling hands and holding them in his warm ones, he replied reassuringly:

"I just want to keep us alive the best way I know how. I know it's not good enough, but we have to try. That's why we have to practice extreme caution, wash our hands, wear our masks even though I think plague is not in the air, unless someone has the type that affects the lungs and starts to cough up blood. Now let me show you more of my observations, because you have a keen mind."

Angelika was somewhat more at ease and against her better judgment had drained her glass as well. 'If I could just tell him, that I am not that smart, that I am a glimpse from the future, advanced science and research are not my strong point, it is time, that is on my side, almost three hundred years of it.'

But she could not tell. The good doctor alone would never be able to protect her, if her story would come out, she would be considered a lunatic, perhaps a heretic and be thrown into one of the asylums she had read about in some monstrous tales of the past. Everybody was on edge, questioning beliefs and religious orientation as a cause in this time of death. No one would be able to understand what had happened to her. She had to stay calm and quiet, keep her thoughts and knowledge to herself, for they could surely burn her at a stake as a culprit of this tragedy.

James had not let go of her hands; he was peering intently into her face as if he was searching for answers in her light brown eyes. He was shaking his head from side to side, frowning just a little before he said:

"You are an enigma to me. I wish I could understand your way! I don't get it, you seemed to know things. Where does this knowledge come from? I have watched you with Rose and some of the other patients. You are too young to be that experienced. I cannot put my finger on it. Why don't you at least try to enlighten me!"

She jumped up; shaking his hand grasps off and somewhat angrily replied:

"There is nothing I know about nursing. I am just copying Elsa and Dora because I don't really know why I am here at all."

'Oh no, I think I said too much,' she thought.

"Please let me go! I need to get back to the others."

"Did you not volunteer like your friends here?" James was by now really puzzled.

"Yes and no," was her vague response, "that is all I can say about it, subject closed."

"I am just curious. Don't be angry, because you are such a strange girl, so different from the others."

"Now Dr. James, that was not too original, almost a cliché, an ordinary pick-up line."

"And what would that be? Pray, tell!"

They were bantering back and forth. James was trying to lighten the mood while Angelika was trying not to give herself away. She was thinking. 'Pick-up line, I doubt that they had that word three hundred years ago. That alone might bust my cover.'

James reached again for the brown bottle and beckoned, "How about one more little sip, one cannot stand on one leg alone?"

"Well, if you are sure it's an antidote, I will have just a little more."

"Right now I am not sure about anything," was his dry remark. "It will make you feel better, so you can carry on."

He became very serious, all flirtation forgotten; lines of exhaustion and sorrow were etched deeply in his young face. He suddenly looked so sad, that Angelika felt sorry for him, taking his hands, she said:

"I am so sorry, James, you are carrying a terrible burden, but you are healthy and strong and I think that we will beat this!" Holding his hands she felt none of that familiar sensation signaling weakness and illness.

"There you go again!" He pulled her close, petting her silky hair; he planted a soft kiss on her forehead, like a benediction. Her eyes filled with tears, she was ashamed to shed, so she kept them wide open, so none would escape to give away her emotions. Her voice was shaky and slightly hoarse:

"I better get back to the dorm, before the girls, especially Maria, will be suspicious."

"I will walk with you, since I know how much you enjoy the rats."

When they stepped out into the hallway, Angelika was slightly lightheaded and somewhat wobbly on her feet from all that antidote. James had to hold her elbow to keep her steady. Thankfully there were no rats at that late hour.

"They are probably all in the kitchen at this time, feasting on cook's leftovers."

"Somehow I don't think so, they are deathly afraid of cook, we all have a healthy respect for her."

He accompanied her to her door and then left quickly as not to be seen. Angelika pushed the door open with all her might, since they had stuffed many rags around the bottom to keep out rats.

"It's about time!"

Maria was sitting cross-legged on her bed filing her fingernails.

"Did the good doctor show you all of his research?"

"Come on, Maria, let her be!" Elsa and Dora shouted at the same time. "Only tell if it is something we should learn!"

"I am sure you know all about it, Dora, after all you are the farm-girl!" Maria was not giving up easily. At this point Angelika had not said a word, but Maria's jibes were going too far.

"If you shut up, and give me a chance, I will tell you all about it, but Maria must get her head out of the gutter first. Let me make it clear that there is nothing going on between James and me. It is purely a professional relationship."

"That must be why we smell liquor coming of your breath all the way over here."

At that Angelika turned beet-red; "Alright, he did give me a drink from a brown bottle, Arrak, I believe he called it. Allegedly it's an antidote to the plague."

"It's an antidote to your virginity, darling, a one-way ticket to get under your skirt!"

"Oh Maria, why must you make everything sound so dirty?" Angelika's eyes filled with tears. "There is no use in my telling you anything, if you don't believe me."

Elsa had jumped up, putting her arms around Angelika's shoulders, she crooned:

"Oh for crying out loud, forget about her, she is just jealous. I believe that you are a good girl and tomorrow I will get us some of that antidote from Mr. Paulus, I am sure he can spare a bottle or two."

After Angelika had calmed down, Dora had put on the kettle to brew a pot of tea and was busy pouring it into five cups. She picked up her mug and seated herself next to Elsa on her bed. They looked over to Rose's corner, only there was no Rose, just a clean bed with fresh linen.

"To Rose!" Dora pointed into the direction of the empty bed with her tea cup.

"To Rose!" they all chimed in, while the fifth cup remained on the table as a sad reminder.

"Now tell us about this research!"

Angelika had put her cup down and while all eyes were hanging expectantly on every word, she tried to explain everything James had told her. About the findings of immunity in the fat rats compared to the skinny ones and how he had compared it to the disease in people. She did not tell about the ledgers in Arabic or about the Jews or Paracelsus. She did not want to shed a light on the science of bacteria and viruses, for her own knowledge seemed too limited to her. Rose's fear stricken eyes and her venomously hissed, 'witch' was still fresh in Angelika's mind and she was frightened. As much as she admired Dora and Elsa and trusted James, she could not be sure how they would react, if they knew the truth and her secret. What she did tell was the fact that James had stressed the importance of hand washing, cleanliness and protection. She also told them, that he did not believe that this disease came out of the air, contrary to what everybody else was teaching. He was convinced that it jumped from rats to people and then again from people to people. She told them about his theory of fleas having a role in that transmission. Elsa was shaking her head almost the whole time Angelika was speaking;

"But how does it start? It has to come from the air, which is why we use incense to purify it."

Dora interrupted:

"Rats have fleas, so do dogs and cats and if you have ever been bitten by those, you know that they jump on people too and those bumps itch forever. One has to wonder, if these fleas carry even smaller animals on them. But would it not make the flea sick as well? So the flea would have to die first, end of story."

Elsa had listened carefully to Dora's explanation and continued her thoughts:

"Even if some fleas die, there are thousands more which could carry on, besides the rats could already be infected. Perhaps the people have been bitten by rats!"

By now they were checking each other for fleas. Angelika was sure she was flea bitten all over; everything was itchy from all that flea and rat talk. They checked their beds, combed their hair, shook out their clothes and were happy to report that they did not find a single culprit. Maria who had listened carefully, but had not participated in their frantic flea search, continued to file her nails calmly. She finally looked up and declared:

"I think you are all crazy! Who has ever heard of tiny animals on fleas? The miasma is in the air, everybody knows that and it is caused by evil spirits among us!"

The last four words, 'evil spirits among us' were spit out between clenched lips while she looked directly at Angelika.

Dora put a protective arm around Angelika's shoulders as if she could protect her from Maria's venom.

"Why do you have to be so mean, Maria?" she hollered.

"The idea of tiny animals on fleas makes more sense than bad air any day! You are just jealous that she caught James's attention. Had it been you, he had given a little antidote to; you would have changed your tune. Oh Maria you are so transparent, it's pathetic."

Angelika was worried that the girls would get into a serious fight. She jumped on her bed to gain some height and lifting her arms, she declared:

"Peace! Let there be peace! It is not important who gets the antidote. It's all just a theory. The Arrak won't fight this disease any more than this tea here, once a person is sickened."

She picked up her mug and in a conciliatory move went over to Maria, handing her a mug as well, "Cheers, Maria, let's be friends, for this might be over soon enough for all of us, one way or another!"

"Listen to the voice of reason!" Elsa lifted her mug in agreement.

Maria could not be swayed. She remained rigid on her bed, stone-faced, ignoring the peace offering of the other three.

"I wonder who will be next," she added in a dry and unemotional tone of voice.

"Do you think Rose is doomed too?" Elsa asked tearfully.

"I do, Elsa," was Mary's short reply.

"Or should we ask our resident psychic here?" She pointed viciously at Angelika, who had tried desperately to ignore her. She had undressed, washed quickly in her basin and had fled under her covers.

"Leave her be!" Dora commanded sternly.

"There is nothing any of us can do to change it. What we can do, is be kind to one another and help each other to get through this. End of story! And now we need to sleep, tomorrow is another day."

They all climbed under their blankets. Elsa blew out the single candle on the table before she also hopped into bed. While each prayed their own prayer to be given strength for the next day, Maria laid wide eyed on her bed, her mind reeling:

'There is something not right with this Angelika and the others are too dense or too naïve to notice that this unusual person has been smuggled right into our midst. Her ignorance about the simplest things is an act. I can feel it. I wonder if she is the cause of all this evil around here. Stranger things have happened,' she thought. She recalled an incident that happened in her small town when she was a child.

It was about the appearance of a young beautiful dark-haired woman. People said that she was a gypsy, shunned from her clan because she had lain with a man other than her husband. Besides adultery she was also accused of having the 'evil eye'. The woman, her name was Clarissa, had found employment on a poor farm outside of the town as a house and milk-maid. They did not pay her but instead abused her with hard labor from dawn to dusk seven days a week for a shoddy room under the eaves of the farmhouse and the left-over scraps from the table. After the spring season with little rain and the beginnings of a hot summer with even less; the fields dried up, the meadows yellowed and the prematurely dried grass crunched under foot. Cows started to give less milk and after a few weeks stopped altogether. Even though the weather abnormality had affected the entire region, people started whispering and then talking behind each other's back about this curious dark haired woman. It did not help that the woman's pregnancy became obvious after a few months and accusations grew louder from day to day. The trifecta of unusual heat, dried up crops, and milk-less cows, drove the ignorant farmers to action. The die was cast:

'She, the woman, the stranger, must have caused these events with her evil eye. She had to go.'

The people she worked for, who were as ignorant and poorer than most, saw a good thing in the hard working slave they had acquired and weakly tried to defend her; afraid to lose such good and cheap labor. They begged the town fathers to leave her alone and just let her have her child in peace. They decided to let her give birth and then to drive her and her bastard infant away, since she would then be useless for labor. Everyone thought Clarissa a gypsy witch and avoided her at all cost. They crossed the street when she approached, and store clerks hid when she tried to enter a store, refusing to wait on her. She was unable to make friends and was never seen entering the church, even though no one had officially forbidden it. Once when Maria and her sisters had gone to confession, she saw Clarissa kneeling in the back pew with her hands folded, weeping silently into her handkerchief. Maria was so moved by the sight, that she asked her mother why everybody was avoiding her. Her mother gave no answer only the stern advice that it was nobody's business. Maria was only a child and did not ask any more questions. In time Clarissa was forgotten: out of sight out of mind, good riddance in the eyes of the good burghers. Many years later, Maria now grown up was told the rest of the sordid and sad story of Clarissa.

While the town fathers were eagerly searching for a way to expel Clarissa from their neat little town, Clarissa's time came when her child was to be born. The dry hot summer had turned to fall, again not enough rain fell to make up for the summer's drought; apples, pears and plums were puny, shriveling on their stems from lack of water, only to drop from the trees during hot breezes like empty shells littering the coarse brown fields below. There was not much of a harvest and people became more desperate than ever. Clarissa by now heavy with child could not work as hard as she did before. This earned her even more abuse and less food from her masters.

During the first frost and heavy snowfall, she was gripped with labor-pain; unable to continue her work, she dragged herself up to her cold chamber under the snow covered roof of the farm house. There she lay on her bare cot alone and unattended for two days. When her screams became unbearable to the farmer and his wife they stuffed cotton-wool into their ears, but did nothing to aid her.

After the screams had turned to moans and eventually to silence for about a half of a day, they decided to climb up the stairs to their cold garret to check on her. It was a pitiful sight. Clarissa lay pale and dead in a large pool of congealed blood. The infant daughter just as pale, lying dead between her legs strangled by the umbilical cord, which was wrapped twice around the infant's neck. While the farmer's wife crossed herself from self-pity, no doubt, and fear of catching evil from the sight of those two beautiful dark angels, for they were absolutely beautiful in their paleness and unworldly peace, the husband called the priest.

He came and purified the room and blessed the dead. Two grave-diggers buried her and the child at the edge of the cemetery outside of its hallowed ground. It was all done quickly and thoroughly under the seal of darkness and silence. The priest did not bless her grave, for she was not of his flock, thank God! One of the grave-diggers was moved with pity for this poor soul and fashioned a small cross, which he drove into the ground at the head to mark the spot. It said: 'Here lies Clarissa, a woman and her child, may she rest in peace.'

For the town fathers it was the solution they had hoped for. She was declared a witch for causing mayhem and a failed harvest, a perfect explanation for the demeaning end of her short life.

By the time Maria was old enough to hear of Clarissa's sad end, the cross had weathered, the script faded but still legible. Someone had planted a red rose behind the old cross, which bloomed in excess just about all year around. Even in the depth of winter, when one was walking around the periphery of the cemetery, a flash of red would interrupt the pristine white blanket of freshly fallen snow. Most townies would avert their eyes, for the blood-red flash of frozen rose petals bore a constant reminder of their sin. These were Maria's last thoughts before she also drifted off to sleep.

Angelika reminded Maria of Clarissa. She was also popped into their midst, seemingly out of nowhere. Anytime Maria had asked her mother about details of the story of Clarissa, she was usually rebuked: "Let well enough alone, there is no use in bringing up ancient history!"

Maria never failed to notice how uncomfortable her mother and everybody else would become, any time Clarissa's name was mentioned. Somewhere in the back of Maria's suspicious and quite jealous mind, she knew that she did not want to make the same mistakes the folks in her town had committed.

Too soon it was morning. The bell rang and the four girls jumped up and into their clothing which had been laid out the night before. Maria walked over to Angelika's side of the room and whispered, "Can I speak to you in private?"

Angelika was surprised, but Maria did look genuinely contrite: "I am sorry about my behavior and my suspicions last night. I know, you mean well and it is altogether your business with James."

"Apologies accepted," Angelika said, "I really just wanted to help."

She did not say anything about James, for she did not trust her voice. Maria hit too close to the truth there and she had to be careful, that none could read the poker-face, she feared she did not possess. Granny always told her exactly what she was thinking just by peering into her eyes. But then Granny was a different story altogether. So they shook hands and with a slightly lighter heart, Angelika and the girls went downstairs for breakfast to strengthen themselves for another grueling day. Cook had laid out a fine array of breads and jams and boiled eggs. 'If only their coffee was drinkable,' thought

Angelika. This brewed chicory and malt abomination colored with milk and sweetened with sugar did nothing to wake up her spirits. She needed caffeine to put a spring into her steps:

"How about some black tea, dear cook," Angelika was almost afraid to ask, but the acrid smell of the roasted malt nearly turned her stomach. Cook must have been in a good mood, for today a big pot of freshly brewed tea appeared in front of her plate.

"You are so kind, dear cook; I thought I will never get rid of this headache without a good jolt of caffeine!" Angelika burst out thoughtlessly.

"Can you spell that for me 'Caffeine', is that what's in the tea?" Cook was shaking her head, "You learn something every day, don't you," and waddled back into her kitchen.

'I must learn to keep my mouth and my thoughts under better control,' thought Angelika. Right now everybody dug in; famished, trying to store up enough energy for the day, because if yesterday taught them anything they knew there would be no lunch break today.

"How is Rose?" Elsa looked concerned.

"Not too good," was Matron's short answer. "I was with her most of the night. She only fell asleep towards morning. The poor thing had the most terrible dreams. All night long she worried about poisons and potions and witches and curses. I can't understand what makes her worry about these things. She must have read something about it, before she fell ill."

Angelika had planned to visit her first thing, but changed her mind upon hearing Matron's report. She decided to stay away, no use inciting Rose's imagination further. When breakfast was done, the girls went to their previously assigned stations. Angelika was happy once again to be working with Elsa, who's calm and confident nature made her feel like she could be of service as well.

The situation outside their stone walls had worsened. In spite of the guards, desperate people had tried to break down the gates, begging for help for their loved ones. The hospital was filled to the brink. No sooner did a person die; another was moved into his spot. Dr. James reminded them all again sternly about the importance of cleanliness and protection. He did not believe in the black oil cloth coats and helmets worn by the other plague doctors. He stressed hand-washing and a fierce war on rats.

It had only been two days since the rats were seen, but cook claimed that she had killed thousands. Two helpers from town were hired to cart off their bodies to the town dump. Often they were buried right along with their fellow human victims in mass graves outside the walled city. Long lines of desperate town folk had assembled along the back gate, where cook had volunteered for the thankless job of handing out left-overs; bread and soup from the kitchen. She was not a bit afraid to catch the disease, so she claimed, and when one saw her in action, one must agree.

"It's the best I can do, Matron, the poor things, which did not catch it, are starving to death. There is no mercy on this earth," she grumbled under her breath.

"You are doing a fine job, Mrs. Cornelius, no one could do more!" Matron was impressed with cook's fortitude and good will.

Angelika was glad to see that most of her charges from the day before were slightly better. The woman, Marie, had gained a little color. Her fever was down and she asked about her children. Angelika had checked on the children first and was happy to report to Marie that she thought the little girl out of danger. She was not sure about the boy. He seemed slightly worse, but when she felt his pulse and checked for fever, he pushed her hand away with some strength, which seemed encouraging.

"He is still hot, but he seems to be a fighter."

This brought a smile to Marie's pale lips. She said with a weak and raspy voice:

"I don't know how to thank you. Without your help, we would have been just as dead as the rest of my family. Maybe there is hope and we get to carry on. God knows, I don't want to be alone. I made a bargain with God; if I survive this disaster, I will spend my days helping these good girls here. I swear, I will learn to become a nurse's helper!"

"Well, that is a good thought, but first you have to get better, and then you have your children to worry about." Elsa had heard the woman's heartfelt promise and smiled.

Marie and her daughter were moved down to the other station, since they did not require constant attention anymore. Two helpers scrubbed the beds and within minutes they were filled again with other casualties. An unconscious girl filled one of the beds. She was the minister's daughter, Minnie, they were told. He had kept her sickness a secret and was hiding her until she fell unconscious. Now scared that she might die without professional help, the minister confessed that she had been ill for two days. He knew that his house would be sealed off immediately, and that the rest of his family, sick or not, were under siege, which meant; isolation and possibly death. He was now unable to minister to his flock, nor enter the church. They were captives of this plague, which did not discriminate between rich or poor, good or bad.

Minnie was pale and her pulse was thready. She was attempting to open her eyes when two masked men pulled off her clothes and put them on the burn pile. She had expensive clothes, made from finely spun muslin with a hand-stitched border, a starched petticoat and soft undergarments. Even the highly polished black buttoned boots were not spared the flames. Those were Dr. James's orders: "All has to be burned!"

She was scrubbed from head to toe and wrapped into a rough linen hospital gown. Angelika checked her groins and arm pits for swollen glands, finding nothing. Her breathing was shallow and labored. Dr. James diagnosed the pulmonic type of the disease.

"She will be coughing blood in no time and then it will be over in about a half day. Please be very careful and wear your mask Angelika, especially when she starts coughing!"

Angelika, who had bathed and changed her, had plenty of chances to have her hands on Minnie's body. All that time she had felt nothing, no tingling, no current, no trembling; nothing.

"I think, she will be alright; no glands, no liver, nothing, just fever!" She ventured to James, who looked up in total surprise, then annoyance, his eyes nearly popping from their sockets:

"And that is your exalted opinion, Dr. Angelika?"

She blushed, feeling heat creep from her face down her neck and beads of sweat pearling on her upper lip and forehead.

'Damn,' she thought. 'Why do I always have to blurt out my thoughts? It's become a dangerous habit.'

"No, James, it's just a feeling I have, nothing else."

"In this place we cannot afford to go by feelings, it's knowledge that's required."

Angelika swallowed and accepted the reprimand. Just then Minnie opened her big blue watery eyes, turned her head to the wall and coughed a thick wad of pink phlegm onto her pillow. Elsa grabbed the masks made from thick gauze and placed them over Angelika's and her own face, before they changed her linen again. But when Angelika turned the hot, feverish body from side to side, there was no sensation. At this point she would have rather bitten off her tongue than make another prediction.

"We just have to wait and see," was Elsa's response. Minnie gratefully closed her eyes and went to sleep. A healing sleep, thought Angelika.

More died, more came. Angelika's back was screaming with pain and her legs were cramping from running up and down the rows of sick people. Hours flew by. Lunch time came and went without a break.

Suddenly the noise outside seemed to be dying down, the rumble of the death-carts seeming further away from the building, when Angelika realized that another day of death and dying had turned to dusk. Matron appeared and summoned the girls to come to supper. Angelika had never been so glad to see a single person before in her life.

They followed the same procedure as the day before; stripping down to their shirt waists, sending all outer clothes to the laundry and dressing in clean skirts and blouses for dinner. Since it was all hospital issue, they all looked alike, a group of single-minded lady soldiers fighting for their lives and those of their charges. James even made them leave their shoes outside. They had to change into funny looking felt slippers at least three sizes too big.

"I guess I am the only one with a size ten, those damn things just fit me fine," laughed Elsa.

Angelika felt like an elf, slip-sliding in her boats, while Maria huffed indignantly, that this was a ridiculous rule, that they would all break their necks and then who was going to take care of that lot out there? That Jimmy-boy needed to have his head examined! Who had ever heard of infected shoes? The man must have lost his mind completely.

Rose had gotten progressively worse over the last few hours. Thankfully Matron had spared the girls this sad news, just told them that Rose was sleeping soundly and not to bother her until morning.

Again cook had laid the table with a great display of roasted chickens, potatoes, and vegetables. Two huge pitchers of ale, their cool exterior, pearling with dew, crowned the splendor.

"How in the world did you conjure up this lovely meal? You have given so much away and roasted chickens, where in God's name did they come from?" Matron could not get over the abundance of food.

"I still have friends in the countryside," said cook. "After I explained about all the good works you people are doing here, my cousin brought these here chickens, half-starved the poor things were after I plucked them, they would have died a natural death soon enough, if you ask me. But after I covered them with thick slices of pork belly and roasted them slowly for hours to get them soft, I figured they was so skinny and old, they needed all the help they can get."

"Well, you have outdone yourself, dear cook and please thank your cousin. His reward shall be in heaven, hopefully not too soon!"

Cook was smiling from ear to ear. Her cheeks, permanently red from the heat of the cooking stove and the little sips of brandy she allowed herself, shone across the table like two rosy apples.

"I think his reward will be here on earth first," she mumbled, not mentioning the fact that the cousin's good will was inspired by a couple of bottles of Mr. Paulus's recipe.

"Let's say a prayer and dig in!" Matron folded her hands and all said a prayer of thanksgiving that they had survived another day. Bowls were passed around and the delicious aroma from the chicken, its fat dripping from the crispy skin made Angelika's mouth water for more. James was busy filling everyone's glass since the pitcher of ale was strategically placed in front of his plate. Angelika sat straight across from him and emptied her mug with one big draught.

"Check out the house chugger!" James laughed and filled her mug again to the brim.

"I am sorry," Angelika stared self-consciously at her plate, "I was so thirsty. We had nothing to drink all day, not even water!"

"And pray tell, who in their right mind would drink water at a time like this. One cannot trust water; it could be infected as well!" Maria could not get over Angelika's stupidity once more.

"She has a point," said James.

"Of course I do!" Maria was shaking her head.

"We drank our water straight from the well, like the animals, none of us ever got sick!" added Dora trying to lighten the tense atmosphere.

"But enough about water; ale is much better, it's nourishing, we all like its effect and it will help us sleep."

"I bet a dose of that antidote is an even better sleep aid!" Maria was baiting James, who had kicked Angelika under the table.

"And how do you know about that, my dear Maria?"

"Well, your precious Angelika was full of it last night and told us all about it."

At this point Angelika's face had turned bright red and she started to sweat.

"What about this antidote, I keep hearing about?" Matron questioned the group. "Is it what Mr. Paulus is fixing for the patients?"

"Not exactly Ma'am, its Arrak, a rum type liquor the sailors drink on their ships during outbreaks of disease." Now it was James's turn to stutter. "At least that's what I read in my old ledgers."

"That's quite interesting, dear doctor and you decided to give some to our little Angelika here?"

"It really was just a little when we were discussing my latest findings."

"Enough talk!"

Matron wanted to change the conversation, since she noticed James's and Angelika's discomfort.

"Let's eat; have more potatoes and gravy, we need to fatten up all of us, it's the only way to survive!"

"Hear, hear," cook lifted her mug high. She was sitting at the farthest end of the table and had listened carefully to the conversation. She had already made up her mind about Angelika and James.

Soon the platters were empty and the pitchers refilled. Cook's apple cheeks positively glowed from the influence.

"I think I got a handle on the rats," she blurted out.

"Put them all in the bin outside, if you want any more there James," she cackled, for she could not for the life of her understand why anybody could be so interested in dead rats. It was a good thing dinner was over when the conversation turned to the rat problem.

James continued kicking Angelika under the table. He had isolated her stockinged legs by dropping his napkin, making a big deal about bending down and picking it up several times. He noticed her small foot in the giant felt slippers and suppressed a smile. Angelika tried to keep a straight face all the while trying to ignore James. Finally Matron got up and took her plate to the scullery. The girls followed suit and offered to help cook with the clean-up, who protested their help:

"You girls run along, you have worked enough for one day. I'll deal with this before I turn in."

"I wish we could take in some air outside. I need fresh air, even if we just open the windows. I think it is now cooler out than in."

James agreed, "Open up, it does not matter; you won't catch death from the air!"

Maria and Dora looked at each other.

"That's what Angelika claims, and we know how much she knows about medicine!"

"Not fair," replied Elsa, "look at the poor thing; all red and bothered, she can't even defend herself! Let's go to our room, open the windows and live dangerously."

"Perhaps Jimmy boy will part with some of that antidote," added Maria.

"Oh Maria, why do you have to twist the simplest thing into ugliness? For a beauty, you sure are venomous!"

Dora admired Maria's beauty, her soft features, dark curls and her sensuous figure, but could not tolerate her meanness.

Dora, strong and capable, could not understand the jealousy Maria displayed when it came to James and Angelika. Dora was sure that she would never be jealous of a man. As a matter of fact, she could not fathom being with one. This was very confusing to her, so how could she ever explain those feelings to another person. She thought of Angelika, who was different from them and so strange, as if she had been dropped into their midst from a different planet. Perhaps she would understand? While the girls continued their chatter, Dora remained deep in her thoughts:

'Perhaps I am a freak of nature; perhaps I should have been born another boy like my three brothers. I am built like them; tall, strong and small hipped. With three brothers I had to fight for everything, food included. Yet I was expected to behave like a girl mainly to marry and bear children. End of story!'

While she blamed her ideation on her upbringing, her disinterest in boys had turned to disgust. It was the single reason why she had volunteered to aid in this epidemic. Perhaps she would contract this, whatever it was and it would be over, all that anxiety and shame.

"You look pensive, Dora", Maria took her hand bending down; she peered into her steady grey eyes. "Is something wrong?"

Maria liked Dora. She was uncomplicated and definitely no competition. Now it was Dora's turn to blush. Maria's hand burned in hers, she quickly drew away and said hoarsely:

"Let's go, I think we are all overwrought and in need of a good night's sleep."

The girls walked down the long hall and started to climb the steps to their dormitory. Angelika was lagging behind when a hand shot out, grabbing her gently and pulling her into a recess of the hall. It was James.

"Meet me in my study; we need to go over some of my papers. I would love to hear your opinion."

"I don't know how I can help you. I just don't know enough."

"Nonsense, you can try. It's your obligation!"

'Obligation' was ringing in Angelika's ears and humming in her brain as she climbed up the stairs behind Elsa.

'Obligation, why me? Oh God, why me?'

Just before dinner James went back to the ward to check on Minnie, the preacher's daughter. Her color was better and her breathing slightly improved. Upon checking and rechecking her groins and armpits, he could not find any swellings. After listening to Minnie's lungs, which he did by leaning his ear directly to her thin chest and back, he thought her lungs somewhat clearer. He was now completely puzzled.

'Could that strange little girl be accurate with her predictions?'

James was perplexed and needed answers before he lost all confidence in his own judgments and diagnosis.

While the girls had made their final round in the courtyard the weather had turned cooler. There was a light breeze which lifted the oppressive heat, even though the walls of the stone building were radiating much of the stored up warmth. Angelika felt as wilted and sweaty as the others and the two big mugs of ale did not cool her down, but instead heated her blood along with the temperature outside, painting her cheeks a most becoming shade of rose.

"I just wish this heat wave would let up. I think it's contributing to the spread of this illness," said Elsa, fanning herself with her hands, "And that stench, it's penetrating these walls here. I can only imagine what it's like outside."

Maria and Dora had skipped ahead and were now waiting at the gate which would let them back through the long hallway to climb the steps to their dormitory.

"At least there are no rats!" Angelika breathed a sigh of relief.

"Cook or Mr. Paulus must have found the right poison, or they all died of plague all at once," was Maria's laconic response.

They were so hot and so exhausted, climbing each step with effort. Angelika hung back thinking how she could possibly explain her escape to have that talk with James. As they entered the room the chance came easily. A note from Matron was laying on the table with Angelika's name on it. It read:

"Angelika, please come and see me in my study as soon as possible!"

"I wonder why she wants to see me. Perhaps I made a mistake, it can't be good!"

Maria took one look at the note. "I find it strange, Matron never sends notes, she comes in person."

"I better go and see what it's all about."

"Perhaps somebody wants to pick that exceptional brain of yours."

Even though Maria had apologized, she could not help her biting remarks. She just was not used to being upstaged at her own game. Elsa had noticed Angelika's stricken face and asked:

"Do you want me to go with you? You have worked alongside of me all day and she can't afford to kill both of us."

"No, it's all right, dear Elsa, whatever it is I can handle it."

While the three busied themselves with the nightly tea preparations, Angelika slipped out. Running down the hall she nearly tripped over one fat healthy looking rat, which eyed her meanly with bloodshot eyes and a twitching tail. She screamed and slammed into the waiting doctor James.

"I can't," she yelled, "I have to see Matron, she sent me a note and I can't stand these creatures. They are evil. Did you see how this fat and filthy thing glared at me?"

"Calm down, first of all, it's not glaring. Bloodshot eyes mean it's almost dead. Look, as we are speaking, it has expired."

The rat crumbled into a heap with frank blood flowing from its muzzle after having a seizure that shook its body violently.

"Oh, I don't care anymore!" Angelika was almost hysterical at this point.

"I just want this whole terrible nightmare to be over. I want to wake up!" She screamed her last words, pummeling James's chest, frightening him as he was trying to calm her.

"There is no note from Matron. I wrote it, because I want you to visit Minnie with me." With that Angelika snapped out of her hysteria:

"Minnie, oh Minnie is going to be alright, or... ?"

"This is what I mean, how did you know? You must understand how this is puzzling me so." James pulled her into his study.

"I hate these oilcloth coats too, but we shall wear them and the masks also, so no one will recognize us as we go back to the wards, breaking one of my most important rules."

The coat was much too large for Angelika and was dragging on the ground. She tripped over it with every step until James took a piece of rope.

"Here tie this around your waist, so you won't kill yourself walking!" he chuckled.

"Well, I am glad I am amusing you, anyway." She was looking down at her person and had to laugh herself:

"A long black coat, a pointed hat, elf shoes, all I need is a broom and my Halloween outfit is complete."

"What the hell is Halloween?"

"Oh never mind, it's nothing!"

James was guiding her along the passageway back to the patients ward. It was quiet now. Guards were at their posts, most of the patients were sleeping and the nuns were whispering among themselves. It was a peaceful scene with few interruptions, a cry here and a moan there, but overall serenity had settled in over the entire ward.

"Those sisters have a special way with the sick. It is another mystery. All they do is pray and lay a cool hand on a sweaty brow and a tortured back and the body relaxes. I have all the medical training and experience, but for the life of me cannot accomplish what they do so simply."

They had approached Minnie's bed. She lay wide-eyed and calm on her pallet, the fever almost gone. Her limbs, which had convulsed earlier, were almost straight and relaxed. She had a sweet smile on her lips once she recognized the pair after they removed their hats.

"She is doing so well, I want to know, why you saw that yesterday, when I was convinced that she was doomed?"

Angelika smiled and took Minnie's hand not only to feel her pulse but to get a good sense of her life force.

"You really are much better, aren't you?"

"Thank you, thank you for all you have done, for I believe, I will live!" Minnie's eyes had filled with tears as she was squeezing Angelika's hands.

"I never doubted it for a minute, but this 'Doubting Thomas' here..." pointing at James.

"If you had it, whatever it is, it was a mild case and you will soon be out of the woods." James was trying to recover some of his authority.

"It does not really matter," a shadow was crossing Minnie's face, "I cannot go home that's for sure. I don't know if anybody is still alive there. You know, they locked the house after I left."

"Since you are doing so well, I'll have cook's friends, the woman just about knows everybody in town, check on your family and give word of your recovery to them."

So a reassured Minnie closed her eyes and drifted off to sleep. James and Angelika waited for a little while and watched her chest moving up and down gently until her breathing became even before they left to go back. Outside they stripped off those offensive coats and shoes and started towards James's study. There they washed their hands very carefully to their elbows in his basin and then splashed them with alcohol.

"Now this did not answer my questions at all," complained the good James. "What is it that you know and feel when you hold their hands? I have observed you and noticed a change in your demeanor depending on the patient. Here let's have some antidote and then you will talk! I won't let you leave until I know the whole story."

He poured her a measure. "Bottoms up!"

Angelika took a big gulp, seated herself into his chair and looked down. Twisting her apron in her hands, she muttered:

"How can I explain myself to you when I don't know?"

Chapter 9

The Truth and Nothing but the Truth, Almost

He sat on the floor in front of her reaching for her hands trying to untwist her apron.

"You know that you can trust me, don't you?"

'How can I trust you when you are not real,' is what she wanted to say. But what is reality? If these last two days have taught her anything, that this particular reality is a shift to a dimension unable to be conceived unless you are caught in its web. How can I tell him about Bella, the rocking chair, Granny, Grandpa, automobiles, modern techniques, not to mention bacteria and viruses without making him doubt my sanity? I cannot take that risk.'

After the second sip he was adamant. "Tell me what you see, because I have seen you in action and it does not add up."

"Nothing adds up, James, so here it is!" She told him about Bella, Granny, herbs and potions and the strange sensation she felt as early as a six year old while visiting the sick with Granny. The more she talked the further he moved away from her, circling her chair, while she was trying to catch his expression as she divulged some of her secrets. She did not tell him about the incredible time shift, for how could he possibly understand it, when she could not. Then she was quiet.

He had finished his drink and was busy pouring another; she had clamped her hands tightly over her glass, too afraid that the liquor would loosen her tongue some more and the rest of the story would pour out unabashed and her stay would become dangerous. He took her hands into his and said:

"So you are one of them!"

"Them! Who? What do you mean? A witch, a saint, touched! What are you trying to tell me?" Angelika's fear was now turning to anger. "That's precisely why I did not want to tell you, it will make it impossible, perhaps dangerous for me to live among the others."

"Calm down!" James was still walking around, his hands clasped around his mug as if he was trying to draw strength from its fiery content.

"My father knew a woman a long time ago; she was a famous herbalist, as good as or perhaps better than Mr. Paulus; a healer and a midwife. She claimed she never lost a mother or a baby in her care. She could predict the outcome of just about any illness we were trying to cure. Much like you she felt a body's life force; either strong or weak or fleeting. She did not know why, only that her mother and grand-mother before her had the same gift or second sight as some called it."

"Was it dangerous for her, did people think her a witch? I know that the church frowns on this gift, call it witchery, blasphemy even heresy!"

"Stop it, though you seem to be quite informed! And that is the other thing. How in the world do you know about things most of us have never heard?"

Angelika just shook her head, unable to answer.

"About the other woman, she was never in any danger, people were in awe of her, hell, they feared her more than the wrath of the church. Since she only used her gift for the good of the community as far as they could tell, they left her alone. My father had the greatest respect for her, he thought her a better healer any day and consulted with her, but always kept her at arm's length."

"How is this supposed to make me feel better, say?" Angelika was about to cry when he pulled her into his arms, pressing her head to his chest, he mumbled:

"Trust me; I will never let anything bad happen to you. I have just one request and please forgive me for asking. What do you feel when I hold you close?"

Angelika's head pressed against his chin and her body was start-ing to mold itself comfortably to his lean frame. They stood like this for some time, before she looked into his face and replied with a very serious expression:

"Do you want me to be honest? Can you handle my prediction?"

He paled, pushing her away and stuttered, "Just give it to me straight!"

"As you wish sir, I am tingling all over," she said "in the most pleasant way from my head to my toes and I do not think it's the antidote, it's you, James, who has me bewitched!" She stepped back and gave him her most angelic smile.

"You are a terrible person," he snorted, laughing with relief. "How can you make fun of this situation, seriously, how can you?"

He pulled her to him again and before she could react, he kissed her hard and deep on her lips. When she opened her mouth to protest, he took the opportunity and probed her tongue with his so that pleasure flooded her so sweetly that she forgot to clamp down her teeth, but let his warm tongue tease hers and explore gently the inside of her lips and cheeks, a sensation she had never felt before. It made her back weak and her knees so shaky that he felt her trembling and lifted her onto his lap before easing both of them into his easy chair. The kiss had made them breathless and after a while coming up for air and back to their senses, they were stunned by their reaction.

Angelika had a hard time sorting out her feelings. 'Was this real? It surely felt real, the moisture collecting deep down felt real. He certainly seemed to be flesh and blood and more. How could she justify this and let it continue?' Her brain was in uproar, thoughts and sensation, conscience and pure animal instinct in an unfair battle for survival. She did not get any more time to think, for he kissed her again and this time not teasingly, but deeper and demanding. When they separated, he eased her gently off his lap, walked over to the door and bolted it shut. She stood nearly paralyzed with fear and also expectation in the middle of the room.

"Are you ready for this?" he asked her gently.

She could not talk, but nodded like an idiot; she thought.

He led her to the small cot under the window and from then on everything became a blur. The white nursing uniform and her underwear were discarded and fell around them like freshly fallen snow. She fumbled with his buttons until he helped her and their bodies melted into one another. There was only a moment when she thought about repercussions, but the moment passed. Her apprehensions about the imperfections of her body, her too small breasts, the fleshy patch across her abdomen and her legs she found too skinny, were kissed away. It was magic, a perfect symphony of pleasure and abandonment performed so expertly, that she hardly felt the pressure and initial pain before it turned to delight!

Later he refilled their mugs and lifting them high, he announced, "To life or what's left of it!"

Her legs were still shaky when she climbed back into her clothes, one last kiss and the bolt was moved. With trembling legs she walked out into the hallway, finding her way back to the dorm. He wanted to escort her, but she thought it wise to go alone. It was late; hours ago she responded to 'Matron's note' and now everyone was asleep. When she opened the door, giving it a hardy push, it creaked and Maria opened first one eye and then the other:

"My, my Matron must have had a lot to talk about."

"Oh go to sleep!" Angelika was too tired and in no mood to defend herself. She walked over to her bed and dressed as she was, climbed under her covers to shut out the world. Once she stretched out, she tried to relive the blissful sensation from earlier but could not. She felt a throbbing pain where pleasure had been just a little while ago bringing with it a nagging sense of guilt and shame. She tried to console herself that this was a dream. 'I am not really here, alive in 1679, so this must also be part of it.'

Before she dropped off to sleep, she bravely reached down between her legs where the slight pulsing continued and felt slick moisture on her fingers. A pale light fell through the wooden shutters of the window, illuminating her outstretched hand. There was a ruby red shimmer glistening in the moonlight. Her last question: 'How can this and this feeling be an imagination?' remained unanswered, before she fell into exhausted slumber.

Morning came too soon. Day three started like the other two. After rushing into their clothes too tired to speak, they took their turn in the privy, where Angelika, after examining herself, found everything back in order. At the breakfast table after Matron had said the prayer, she added with a serious tone that they all needed to see Rose first, who was worse again at night. The attending nuns had called Matron several times during the night, for Rose's ravings had become too much for the sisters.

"Your name came up several times, Angelika. She kept asking for you and then she wanted me to stop you or get you. I could not understand all of it. I thought you two hit it off right away. I know that she is your special friend!"

Angelika could not believe her ears. She thought. 'That's it, she will openly accuse me.' Out loud she said:

"Perhaps I shall go and see her by myself first. If she wants to talk, it might be easier done in private."

Not waiting for Matron's permission, she jumped up and headed for the door. Her appetite was gone and she did not mind missing breakfast and especially the looks and whispers from the other girls.

She found Rose in the back of the ward among the sickest, the ones Matron had under her care. She could not believe her eyes when she realized how wasted Rose's little body had become in just three days. She seemed to be sleeping, but when Angelika approached the bed; her eyes popped open and attempted to focus. In spite of Angelika's coverings and mask Rose recognized her and opened her mouth in disbelief croaking:

"Have you come to finish me off?"

Angelika sank down on the floor next to her cot clasping Rose's claw-like icy hand into hers, she whispered:

"Rose, please listen to me, I am your friend. I would make you better if I could. You were already sick before you came. Remember how weak you felt and how you could not eat?"

Rose was trying to pull away with all her strength, but Angelika held on:

"You must believe me, Rose, I wish you no harm. I am not a witch. I am just not from your time and I myself do not know why and how I came to be here."

Rose's bright green eyes had not lost their intensity when she turned her full attention on Angelika's face. Green eyes burning amidst blood red sclerae into brown ones!

Angelika did not have to touch Rose to see that her end was near. She got even closer to Rose, lifting her shoulders off the bed to ease her breathing and clasping her into her arms as if she was trying to wrestle her away from death; away from the reaper, who had shown her no mercy. As Rose's breathing eased, her gaze never left Angelika's face and then suddenly like a ray of sunshine fallen through a leaden sky, she smiled and focused her eyes for the first time beyond Angelika, beyond this ancient ward with its grey walls and merciless pestilence and her mouth formed these words softly and clearly:

"Angelika, I am sorry, now I see!" The light broke in her eyes, her body relaxed with a deep exhaling breath and then it was over. Rose was gone.

Angelika eased Rose's body back onto the cot and covered her with a sheet. While she was still on her knees reciting her prayer, James approached the bed. Seeing the still and covered form of Rose, he also lowered himself onto his knees next to Angelika and took her into his arms. She sobbed quietly against his chest and for the second time in three days felt safe, like she had come home. The feeling was good but again confusing. They rose together and decided to take the sad news back to the others in the dining hall. The burning question remaining in her mind; 'Who will be next and how many will have to die before I am allowed to go back?' was not answered. 'Perhaps by the end of this third day this mystery will be solved. Three has always been the magic number. People get buried after three days; the magic three, the Holy Trinity, God the father, Jesus his son and the Holy Ghost. Jesus rose after three days. The structure of life, the inner, middle and outer leaves of all that lives, snowflakes, three leaf clovers, even the wicked poison ivy grows from three leaves. It has been said that death always claims three. Who will be next? Dora, Elsa, Maria or I?'

Once they entered the dining hall, they did not have to say a thing. All could read their expressions. Elsa and Dora started to weep, while Maria just stared stone-faced into her lap and questioned Angelika,

"What did Rose say at the end, did she speak?"

"She smiled and said, "I see.""

"Well, that is quite unsatisfactory," mumbled Maria. "I thought she had you figured out."

"Perhaps she knew at the end, that she was wrong." Angelika was getting sick and tired of Maria's continuous attacks.

Even James noticed the hostility in Maria's voice and, clapping his hands, announced:

"It's time! Everybody to their posts; Matron and I will sort out what needs to be done about Rose. We will give notice to her people. They won't be able to fetch her, but at least they can pray for her, if they are still alive."

Rose's death had put an added damper on the already strained atmosphere and thin peace among the girls. Only cook seemed unperturbed:

"It's God's will," she said crossing herself repeatedly, "her suffering is done, so we have to be happy for her and not pity ourselves over her loss."

Elsa and Angelika went back to their assigned ward. They were relieved to find that most of their charges had been transferred further down the aisle, a sure sign that they were on the mend. Marie was well enough to get up and care for her little boy. Her daughter was not fairing as well, but Angie still could not find any swollen glands, just a high fever and lethargy. She was almost positive that she did not have the same disease as her mother and brother and said so to Dr. James:

"Here you go again, Angelika, what you think?" he was looking intently at her handling the small child.

"Nothing, I feel nothing but a strong will to survive." She smiled up at him, relieved that for the time being, he was prepared to keep her secret.

Angelika had opened the shutters and pushed open the boarded up windows to let in as much fresh air as possible. Matron had placed guards all around the hospital to keep the hordes of the sick and dying away from its walls. As cruel as it seemed to Angelika, she understood that they had to protect those within their walls. The heat wave had loosened its grip and the cool morning air had a fresh sharpness they had not felt in a while.

"It's a good sign," Mr. Paulus said cheerfully as he was stocking their cupboards with a fresh supply of potions and lotions from his apothecary.

"The rats are gone!" proclaimed cook, "I either killed them all or they moved on. Either way; I have not seen a single one this morning."

"The rats are gone; the rats are gone, gone are the rotten things and in comes the sun!" The children were singing and Elsa and Dora were dancing a crazy jig in the aisle between the beds.

"The rats are gone, the rats are gone!"

"Just wait until tonight, we will know by tonight which is their feeding time, if they are truly gone," Maria being the eternal pessimist added.

James and Angelika went to visit Minnie, who was in high spirits, having had good news from cook who knew her father, the preacher, well.

"There were no more new cases of disease in town last night. That's a good sign, isn't it?" Minnie sat in bed bright eyed and ready to go.

"Sorry, my dear," said James, "you will have to stay with us, because your house is still under quarantine, locked up with everyone in it. We still have to wait and hope." He pulled her gently back down on to her pillow. "And you will need your rest until you're fully healed."

Overall the mood had changed. The good news from the town, the absence of rats and the cool breeze which had also cooled their tempers made life more hopeful for the moment. It did little to ease the terrible sadness they all felt over Rose's death.

After their initial chores had been taken care of off they all went to the little chapel area where Matron had taken great pains to present Rose. She had been washed and dressed into a fine shroud. Candles illuminated her pale beautiful face which shone with heavenly peace. While her body had been ravished by disease, her face remained angelic as to remind the others of the greater peace all will experience at some time.

Later they continued working at their stations until all patients were properly taken care of. The dead had been moved out, still others came to fill their space almost immediately, but it seemed as if the urgency had eased. Guards stopped shouting at the gate every time orderlies allowed more of the sick to be admitted. The first three were unconscious when Elsa and Angelika cleaned and dressed them into rough hospital issue shirts. Her hands and arms vibrated with each touch of this last lot and she held out little hope for those new victims. Elsa too could feel swellings everywhere she checked and soon summoned Dr. James.

"These here have to be cut immediately, if they are to have a fighting chance doctor!" she hollered.

"Angelika, get the blade, the basin and the cotton wool for binding the wounds!"

This was the part she hated most of all. Although these patients were already unconscious and beyond reach, she knew the minute that blade would pierce the painfully swollen glands, their eyes would pop open and their mouths and throats would form the most inhuman shrieks her ears had ever heard. James remained unperturbed; cutting away and staunching the flow of blood and puss. While Elsa was holding the basin and passed the cotton, Angelika was holding her ears.

"It's their only chance dear," he muttered concentrating on the task at hand, feeling sorry for the girl witnessing this much misery.

"But it's no use, why hurt them, when they have to die anyhow. Why not let them die in peace with some dignity," Angelika whispered.

"There you go again." James was getting impatient with her attitude when Elsa reminded him that Angelika's predictions up to this time had not failed.

"And why is that, you must tell us!" Elsa was getting more curious by the minute. Angelika was afraid to trust even good-natured Elsa with her secret. Life would become too dangerous, she was certain of it. It was a risk she could not afford to take.

The day passed without further incident. Three of the newly admitted patients breathed their last after a few hours in spite of lancing their boils and bathing them with wine. Angelika's assessment had been absolutely correct once again.

Thankfully cook called them all for dinner. They washed and changed according to the rules and gathered in the dining hall.

Matron had the deepest and darkest circles under her eyes and could not have looked any more distraught, when she announced that Dora did not feel well and half way through her shift had taken ill. She did not have a fever yet, but felt too weak and too nauseated to continue.

"I have put her in with me. I will not take any chances with the rest of you getting more exposure than absolutely necessary."

Angelika could not believe her ears. "Dora, I must see her immediately!" she cried and jumped up.

"Hold your horses, child!" Matron was adamant. "First we eat and drink and then I will allow you and James a visit."

Maria glowered and muttered under her breath:

"James and Angelika! Well there comes the dynamic duo once again to the rescue. Note how well Rose faired!"

"Not fair, Maria!" Elsa grabbed her by the wrist and shouted, "Let it go, we will all get a chance to see her. Stop this negativity, I can't stand it anymore!"

Cook had tried her best to serve up a good meal, but she had to dig deeper into her dwindling supplies, since just about all contact with the outside world had been cut off. She managed to bake a terrific casserole from fatback, beans and potatoes. Preserved plums in Arrak and a healthy shot of Mr. Paulus's antidote became the crowning glory of the meal.

"Goes great with plums, don't you think?" Cook was smiling from ear to ear, popping her rosy apple cheeks out. They started to glow even brighter after a few sips. With all this fatty food Angelika was getting quite immune to the effects of cook's ale, which she now drank for thirst just like the others and had come to rely on the antidote for that pleasant buzz. James smiled at her across the table, noticing her downing that first mug in one big swallow about as fast as the others. However, in spite of the good food, there were no pleasantries exchanged at this meal. Everyone hunched over their plate, eating as fast as possible to get this over with in order to see Dora.

Angelika and James donned their nasty oil coats and made their way to Matron's room. Her heart was beating too fast and too hard as if it tried to jump out her chest and she felt nearly faint with apprehension. Even James looked dead serious and his hand was ice cold as he was urging her along the passageway to the first floor. On the landing a rat crouched against the steps, bleary eyes stared up at them over a viciously hissing muzzle dripping with pink foamy blood.

"So much for the idea, that the rats are gone. This one looks ready to attack, but has no strength left."

"It will be dead, when we return," was James' flat response.

They found Dora bundled up on a cot in the corner of Matron's study. She was pale and cool and had vomited into a basin.

"Well that's it for me, right? I felt all around myself and so far I have found no glands, no swellings in my abdomen, no fever, only over- whelming fatigue. I can't seem to keep anything down. It must be the beginning of the end. Don't come too close, save yourselves!" she cried with tears streaming down her boyish angular face.

Angelika noticed for the first time how attractive Dora was in a spare way.

James countered, "Don't be silly girl; all you have is indigestion, because you don't have any of the other symptoms. We are all so gun-shy right now that every minor ailment is magnified in our minds."

He sat next to Dora on her cot and patted the space beside him for Angelika. She knew what he wanted her to do. The fear of touching Dora and then feeling the vibrations travelling up her arm, telling Dora that the end was near was just too much to ask. So she continued to stand by the door, unable to move closer to the cot.

"Come nearer, she won't bite."

"I might throw up on you though!" Dora was trying to joke and when a small furtive smile washed over her exhausted features, Angelika felt brave enough to get close. That was when Dora grabbed her hand, and pulling her down whispered into her ear:

"Promise me that you will be nicer to Maria; she doesn't mean it, you know!"

Angelika was so taken aback by this remark that she forgot all about tingling and vibrations, but responded angrily:

"Me, unkind, when was I ever unkind? After all the rumors Maria was spreading about me, I had the right to defend myself!"

"Please do not be angry, Angelika. I just have to know that she is ok. I have been watching over her. She just can't help it sometimes. Her mouth runs ahead of her brain."

Looking into Dora's pale and frightened face, Angelika relented somewhat:

"Sure, I promise, but it won't be necessary, you will be there for a long time to protect her. I am sure of it."

James got up and searching Angelika's face, his expression was one big question. He said carefully:

"Dora, dear, you will be alright, you are very strong and I am sure, that you do not have plague." He had read Angelika's expression and knew that she felt no fleeting life.

"Don't ask me how I know, I just do. It will be our secret, promise me."

Weak with relief they all laughed, holding hands while jerking the poor patient up and down in a strange looking jig.

"You get some rest," was James's prescription. "And you will be right as rain in a couple of days. I think you're plagued by cook's generous portions of fatback and beans."

"Oh, don't remind me," Dora was turning a greener shade of pale and reached for her basin.

"I will send you some tea and dry biscuits later," promised Angelika. Outside the door James and Angelika embraced, relieved.

"Do you think that she will keep our secret?" Angelika was concerned.

"I think she will, unless you are not nice to Maria," joked James.

"That is almost impossible, the way she goads me continuously, but I will try. Promise, cross my heart and hope to die!" At that they both burst out laughing. Angelika thought, 'this is what plague does to people.'

The rat on the steps was still glowering at them with bloodshot eyes as they passed it.

"We must tell the others the good news!"

By now they felt such relief they were almost giddy. In the dining hall the crew had just finished their second pitcher when all eyes were directed towards James and Angelika as they entered.

"Good news! She has an upset stomach and will be as good as new in a couple of days!"

"Thank God," they all breathed a sigh of relief while cook quickly filled their glasses with more antidote. Smiling from ear to ear cook cried:

"I guess that old Paulus got it right, the stuff is working, that's why I keep a small stash by my stove." She quickly clamped her hands over her mouth, blue eyes crinkled up over rosy red cheeks. She had said too much, but everyone just clapped and laughed.

"You deserve every drop, my dear cook!" Even Matron was now in a good mood and treated herself to a rare second shot.

Maria still had not said anything. She was, as usual, concentrating on observing James and Angelika. Finally she lifted her mug in a congratulating manner high up into the air and proclaimed in a clear voice:

"And whose diagnosis is this, I might ask? Is it our good doctor's with all of his ledgers and his passion for cleanliness or that of our foundling, Angelika, who seems to have the knowledge?"

The joking and the laughter stopped and all eyes rested on Angelika.

"I am not a doctor," she said in a shaky voice. "I only observe and rely on James here," she ventured, looking uneasy.

"Oh forget it, who cares, the main thing is; Dora is going to be fine!" Elsa the peacemaker took over. Alas, the jocular mood was broken, cook got up to clear the table and Matron stood up, leaning heavily on the table in front of her, declared:

"Good night, good people; have a good rest and I will see you in the morning!" The girls started to walk out together as James called:

"Does anybody want to go outside for a breath of air?"

Angelika stopped and turned around. Without caring what Maria would say, she fell in step with James as they made their way towards the courtyard.

Once they left the passageway and the group behind them, a cool night breeze enveloped them like a healing touch. Angelika took James's hand and without looking at him said:

"Explain to me, what this relationship is about! Is it real or is it imagined? I do feel an attraction to you unlike anything I have ever felt before, but I can't help wondering what this is all about?" What she wanted to say was: 'It cannot possibly be anything but a dream. This started out as a dream, turned into a nightmare and ended in bliss. No wonder I am confused, for I am not like this, never in my real life would I be as easy and free with all I have to give.'

The moon was full; its light brighter and more intense than she had ever seen. She remembered Bella's saying that the weather always changes with a full moon. It must have brought on the first cool breeze, ending the strange heat wave in early spring.

As they wandered through the courtyard past the privy, along the high walls of different shrubs, among them lilac bushes, their blooms, long wilted, pouring their strength into their foliage, creating huge heart-shaped leaves which made a great hiding place for the pair. James pulled her into the shadowy retreat, holding her close; he whispered into her ear, that he was not a dream but a true flesh and blood man, who was totally in love with her. As much as Angelika enjoyed his confession, she could not believe any of it, for she could not understand nor explain this time-shift. She was deep in thought.

'I wonder if I am ever able to explain myself to him, when I cannot grasp this reality myself. I do not know what to do. Oh, please God, Granny, Bella, help!' she prayed fervently to all that was holy to her.

But she was young and nature took over and with her brain muddled with the antidote, her body responded in its natural way. She held on tight to James and molded her body into his embrace. Her head found the comfortable spot in-between his ear and his chest, fitting itself perfectly into this mold. As her body relaxed and her breath became even, she listened to the regular thump of his heart and gave herself over to the feeling of being safely in his arms. She could tell that he was holding back emotions he also was not familiar with, by the slight tremble of his embrace. Or was it she who was trembling?

They stood like this for some time until fatigue overwhelmed her. Yawning, she begged to go back.

"I must get some rest, if I am going to survive another day in this ancient hellhole." She swallowed the last word.

"I am sorry dear, I lost track of time and I keep forgetting how hard you girls have to work."

Slowly they walked back to the gate entering the passageway which was now deserted by rats and humans alike.

"You better go, I'll find my way, the moon is so bright, I won't even need a candle."

As they passed the privy, Angelika checked in, while James waited patiently outside.

"I'll never get used to this! Just for this alone I wish I could just wake up. I swear, I will never take a real toilet and running water for granted as long as I live," she swore under her breath.

"What are you mumbling?"

"Oh nothing, just how much I hate this privy."

"Well, it's the best we have, beats a chamber-pot any day!"

That last remark made her laugh out loud.

"What is so funny about that?"

"Perhaps I'll get to explain it to you some time, soon I hope!"

They had reached the stairway to her dorm room. He pulled her into his arms for a last embrace and kissed her lightly on her lips.

"Good night, my mysterious fortuneteller," he whispered and turned to leave.

When Angelika opened the door to their room, her face flushed and her eyes bright, Maria and Elsa were sitting quietly at the table. Elsa made tea and was in the process of pouring it into three mugs:

"I am glad that you are back. Here, have a cup and when we're done we will read the leaves." Maria was crouching on her bed; she did not miss Angelika's flushed appearance and light mood.

"Well, I'll say, the good doctor is definitely improving your complexion!"

"Oh, lighten up, Maria! I like him and he likes me. It will all be over soon enough. I'll be gone and then everything will be back to normal around here!"

"And pray where will you be going too, if I might ask?"

"Oh, I don't know, just gone from here, back to where I belong and there will be no Doctor James, I can assure you of that!"

Angelika had said these last words which such emphasis and conviction, that Elsa looked up in surprise, but Maria clamped her lips together and kept quiet, which was the response Angelika had hoped for. After the tea was drunk, they stared at the bottom of their mugs where a few leaves had gathered in the shallow pool arranging themselves into their predestined shapes.

"I can't make out what mine are trying to do; they are still floating as if an unseeing hand is keeping them from settling. It is as if they are having a life of their own." Angelika was staring into her mug in surprise for she sat still and had not moved the container. Elsa, who knew all about tea leaf formation, leaned over and exclaimed:

"It looks like they are trembling; perhaps the whole house is shaking a bit."

"There is no wind and nobody is shaking!"

Maria had moved over to the table as well. Six eyes were staring into Angelika's mug, watching tea leaves dancing a strange jig before they settled into an intricate pattern on the sides of the cup, leaving the tiny pool of tea at the bottom empty.

"Well, I'll be," Elsa cried. "I have never seen anything like this before. Not a single leaf left at the bottom, just a murky splash. How did it get so cloudy? The tea we drank was clear."

Tea leaves were clinging to the sides in no particular pattern until their trembling formed them into half-moons, with one exception; a single leaf had leapt from the pool and perched precariously on the rim of the mug.

"That is you, Angelika!" Maria exclaimed, "Not belonging and trying to leave."

"Well, we won't let her." Elsa had taken Angelika's hand. "We have to be strong; there's only the three of us now."

The tea leaves in Maria's cup showed the shape of a bird, its wings spread wide.

"What do you think of that, Elsa?"

"It's an eagle, Maria! Proud and strong and beautiful like you, above all and larger than life. It is a good sign."

Lastly they concentrated on Elsa's cup. Her leaves had not settled, but floated happily on the clear pool of tea. They had plumped up and made no pattern at all.

"There is too much water."

Elsa reached for her cup and took another tiny sip. Once she set the mug down, the tea leaves formed a perfect circle with one single bit floating in the middle. Elsa looked astonished into her cup.

"There is another first; a perfect circle. I shall call it the 'Healing Circle' with one amiss, who must be Rose."

"Oh stop it," Maria cried. "You are giving me goose-bumps. It's only a game, a stupid fortune teller game. Tea cannot foretell the future, nor explain the past. Let it be!" Without further ado she took all three mugs and emptied them vigorously into the basin.

"I still do not understand why Angelika's tea was murky. She did not use sugar. It was the same brew as ours." Elsa was contemplating this point, but Angelika knew the answer. It was the mystery she was unwilling to share at this time. It was the last thought she had before they all crawled under their blankets to go to sleep.

"Good night Angelika, thanks for the good news about Dora," Maria sighed and then there was silence.

Chapter 10
The Third Day

Three days had passed in which agony as well as ecstasy were relieving one another in a crazy dance.

Angelika's hope that day three would bring resolution to her dilemma vanished. There it was morning again, the bell ringing its caustic shrill ding announcing another round of more sadness or perhaps bliss? Tired of relying helplessly on a fate she did not believe in, she decided to take matters into her own hands

'This is the day I am going to take my life back, come hell-fire and brimstone, the end of the world or perhaps my life as I know it. I will be going back!' She swore under her breath as she made her hasty ablutions once again with cold water from her basin and then climbed into a clean dress and apron. 'I will finally show them what I am about. If they kill me, so be it, for the plague will get us soon enough. I have had enough of death and dying and foremost of lying.' That she promised herself.

All the others were just as weary as Angelika, still tired and with sore muscles from the last day's work, as they approached the breakfast table. Elsa could barely keep her eyes open. Maria tried unsuccessfully to appear groomed and proper for the day ahead. She had pinched her high cheek bones furiously, but it was of no use. Instead of her usual rose blush she had created only red pinch marks on an otherwise deathly pale face. She had lost weight. Her skin was pulled tight around her facial bones off-setting her jet-black curls which lay lusterless in spite of vigorous brushing. Matron could not have looked worse for the wear, even James appeared listless. Only cook showed some vigor by chatting them up cheerfully:

"Come my beauties, sit down; there will be eggs and bacon, fried bread and applesauce."

A huge steaming pot of tea appeared in front of Angelika and James. Cook remembered how Angelika loathed that hot malt beverage. She had really made an effort, but could not rouse their enthusiasm. The idea of more fat back bacon and fried bread brought nausea to rise in the back of Angelika's throat:

"Just tea and plain bread for me, please! I think I have to stay away from that bacon."

"Nonsense, my dear, look at you, nothing to you! A good wind could blow you over. It's the fat that keeps you going all day!"

Maria also stared at her plate as if she was served vermin. Only Elsa, good old chunky Elsa, ate with some appetite, thinking that it will be a long time until dinner. James looked at Maria with some concern.

"How are you this morning? Looking rather peeked!"

'Peeked is not the word,' Maria thought, but answered with strained effort, "Just perfect as always, ready to go!" It was not in Maria's personality to give in so easily. She would pretend and look good until she dropped.

After breakfast they took a tray to Dora, who had had a wonderful night's sleep in Matron's study. She looked bright-eyed and nearly restored as Elsa was setting the tray down. Cook made her a special tea and a big bowl of oatmeal with honey. Angelika, who detested oatmeal under normal circumstances, thought that it looked more appealing than that tedious fat back. She bent down to grasp Dora's hand and felt only the vigorous pounding of her pulse with returning strength. James followed the girls and was trying to read Angelika's expression as she was holding Dora's hand. After he bent down, pressing his ear to her chest and back, listening to her breathing, he gave a big smile and declared:

"You are on the mend my dear!"

"I feel absolutely fine, I look better than all of you put together," she laughed. "I had one day of rest and it shows. You all look like hell, especially Maria!"

Maria's pale face had turned a crimson color. It was hard to tell whether she was feverish or angry or both. James noticed it too and pulled her aside. After putting his hand on her forehead where little beads of sweat were forming, he looked concerned and said, "Maria, Maria, you are burning up. Let's give you Dora's cot here, since she appears quite recovered!"

Dora jumped up and grasped Maria's shoulders forcing her to sit on the side of the cot.

"I am fine, stop making a fuss. I am only tired and this hot tea of cook's made me blush. I wonder what special wake-up herb she used to make her morning blend? I would not be surprised if she put a shot of Mr. Paulus's antidote in it. I got hot right after drinking a few sips."

"Strangely it did not affect the rest of us that way." James was shaking his head from side to side and looked intently at Angelika. She knew what he wanted her to do, but she would not, could not touch Maria. It was too painful and frightening. While James and Angelika were caught up in their silent game of assessing each other's intuitions, Elsa took charge:

"Hot tea or not, you look ill!" She pushed Maria down on Dora's cot and started to take off her shoes, her apron and loosen the collar around her neck to give her more air. "You are hot, girl," she mumbled as her hands brushed Maria's face and arms.

The minute Maria laid down, her eyes closed and she gave in to the weakness, whispering, "This is good. I will rest a while and then I will be good as new." She buried her head into Dora's pillow and seemed to be fast asleep almost immediately.

"Let her rest and I will check on her later," James ended the visit and the speculations for the time being.

Elsa and Angelika took up their duties at their station, where conditions had further deteriorated. Some patients from the day before had died; others took their spot during the night and looked worse this morning. One of them was a porter, who for the last three days, had faithfully brought in the sick and carried out their bodies after they died. He was crazed with fever; black spots covered his face and chest and his swollen and lanced buboes had saturated their cotton wool bandages.

"Let's start with him!" Elsa was eager to get the worst over with; this porter deserved their attention first since he had been a faithful servant.

"It's not fair," mumbled Angelika under her breath as she held his feverish flailing body while Elsa changed the dressings. "There is nothing fair about this disease," said she. "It strikes the rich and the poor alike, the good and the bad without care."

"Not true!" argued Angelika. "The rich always have a way out, they pay their way out of places of misery, while the poor are stuck with no place to flee, no place to hide. Most of the town fathers, the rich merchants and even most of the doctors have fled. It is what cook told us days ago. They fled this sinking ship like the rats they are."

Elsa listened to Angelika's frustrated ranting and added:

"They won't get too far; there will be an infected rat for each one of them as well. But I do agree that it is almost always better to be rich than to be poor."

The whole unit looked bleak and hopeless even though news from the outside had improved. The rats seemed to be gone for now and no new cases had been reported.

"I wish we could open the shutters." Angelika was tired of the hot fetid air in the ward. 'No wonder they think that this illness comes from the air. By now I feel the same way.'

When Matron approached, the girls pleaded with her to open the shuttered windows for some fresh morning air. "The crowds are gone outside, it is safe."

Surprisingly Matron agreed. She also did not believe that this disease came from the air. She had been around too long and had seen too much to give credit to those 'old wives' tales. She had many discussions with various physicians, some of whom still believed in curses and witchcraft, but many studied the sick and much like Dr. James had their own theories of a different source of contamination. Even though there was no real prove as of yet, many believed that there had to be a middleman to transmit this disease so efficiently. So why not blame the rats?

The windows had been bolted shut and it took several men to break through the barriers; pushing out those offensive boards and letting in fresh air and sunshine. Everyone took a deep breath. The morning air was still cool and smelled sweetly of wilted lilac and crushed rose petals. Even the sickest in the ward relaxed their facial features, which had been drawn into a grimace for so long, when the sweetly scented breeze caressed their tortured limbs and faces.

Angelika and Elsa stepped up to the window opening and took deep filling breath in through their noses and out through the mouth. After a short while they also felt refreshed and almost renewed before returning to their tasks at hand.

Since no more patients came in, they decided to check on Maria. They took the back steps to Matron's study, after removing their aprons and scrubbing their hands and arms according to James's instructions.

Maria appeared to be sleeping restlessly, turning from side to side. Her face was bright red. Sweat was pouring from her body and she was muttering incomprehensibly. Elsa sat next to her on the cot and grasped her hot hands:

"Sh, Sh, Sh", she crooned. "Calm down, we are trying to help you."

Angelika stood mortified at the door. She could not force herself to come any closer. 'This is a repeat of Rose's story', she thought. 'Why Maria? She is so capable and so proud.'

Elsa beckoned her to come closer and try to figure out what Maria was saying, "Come close, I cannot make out what she wants!"

Even though Angelika was scared to death, she squatted down next to the cot, when Maria cried out and, half way sitting up, grabbed Angelika's arm. Her eyes were not focusing, but were moving from side to side in their sockets as if they were searching for a focus point. With a death-grip on Angelika's arms, she pulled her all the way down, so close that Angelika could smell her fetid breath, and whispered:

"It's you; I knew that I would be next!"

Angelika was trying to unclasp Maria's grip on her forearm, when she became aware of the familiar vibrations and tingling traveling up her arm straight to her heart. She gasped in surprise and horror, for she could not deny the sensation.

"What is it?" Elsa noticed Angelika's frightened face and pallor.

"Oh Elsa, I am so sorry, I am almost positive that she has it!" she whispered softly behind her hand, but Maria's eyes flew open, locked with Angelika's and while she let her tense body relax into the pillow, she muttered:

"It's alright; I knew it would end like this, the minute I laid eyes on you!"

Elsa, who overheard every word responded sharply:

"Enough already, this is pure nonsense, both of you, stop it! Even if you have it Maria, you will survive. You are not Rose, who was a fly-weight. You are strong and sturdy; no amount of little plague is going to undo you. End of story! Now I do not want to hear about what you know; pointing at Maria, and about what you feel; nodding into Angelika's direction. Now I will get James and he will decide what is to be done."

Maria closed her eyes and seemed to fall asleep during Elsa's outburst. Once they left the room, they fell into each other's arms and started to sob:

"I am telling you, she is worse off than you think," Angelika cried into Elsa's shoulder.

"Well, you have not been wrong yet, but there has to be a first time." Right now Elsa decided for all of them, that the power of positive thinking would give Maria strength to survive. They walked back down to the ward and gave James the bad news.

"Hell and damnation!" was all he could say, shaking his head; he left them to check on Maria so he could form his own opinion.

The news of Maria's sickness spread quickly to the others. Dora was helping cook in the kitchen first, before going back to the ward. Angelika found them sitting around a huge bowl of potatoes, which they peeled while shaking with laughter from one of cook's jokes. Dora could not believe her ears. She was speechless, while cook grabbed a white handkerchief and started to dab at her puffy little eyes which usually sparkled with mirth inside their well upholstered orbits. In another minute they all cried, tears mingling freely with the cloudy potato water.

"Oh God, not our Maria," cook was getting hysterical. "She is so strong and so beautiful, her poor parents," she wailed.

Angelika was trying to calm them down. "You know there is a chance she will get better, some do beat this. Let's see what James finds out!"

She did not tell them about the vibrations she felt and how fleeting Maria's pulse had been. She knew that there was little strength left in her and she was not sure about Maria's will to fight. Something far beyond was beckoning. Maria was listening and Angelika knew it, even though she was unable to see beyond this veil. There was nothing else to be done but to go back to work. James joined them there. His facial expression seemed grimmer than ever.

"I still can't believe Maria is coming down with this. She must have already been infected before she came, since it's only been three days. No glands yet, which is surprising, we will see tonight. Angelika, you and I must speak!"

"Oh no James, please we have way too much to do here. Elsa cannot spare me for a minute."

Elsa had also observed James's expression and, but as clueless as she was, she agreed with him:

"That's ok Angelika, you run along, I can manage, but bring me back a nice cuppa… from cook, will you, be a lamb and run!"

James started to laugh at her and with a little twinkle in his bright blue eyes and joked:

"See, even Elsa knows what's best, let's go and bring back that nice cup of tea for her." James put his large hand around Angelika's shoulders and more or less pulled her along the passage towards his study or lair, as Angelika started to think about it.

"Please don't press me for information I may not have, I beg you!" Angelika looked helplessly up at James who had pushed her gently into his overstuffed chair.

"I will never get used to the way you speak," he said. "Please just tell me what you felt when you held Maria's hand!"

Angelika sank back into the chair's comfortable stuffing, closing her eyes she felt utterly defeated:

"I will not lie to you. I was literally shaking with dread when she pulled me down. There is not much life left in her, I am sure of it. Glands or no glands, if she does not have plague, she is dying from something else!"

James was restlessly pacing up and down the length of the study. Five steps to the right, five steps back and so on, nearly knocking over the little desk where the bottle of antidote was swaying with his agitated movements.

"What in the name of God are you feeling? All she has is fever and malaise, but there is something else, a desire of letting go, I can detect it myself and I have no such gifts."

"Perhaps she is just tired and the idea of giving up, ending it all is more desirable than living this nightmare!" Angelika was close to spilling her story at this point. She herself felt near the end of her endurance. 'Why now?' she thought.

News from the outside was improving, no new cases were arriving which was a good thing since most of the porters and the gravediggers were dead. There was no wood for coffins to be had. At the last meeting the surviving council members decided to open up 'Plague-pits' so surviving family members could bury their own in mass graves. Unfortunately the pits were exposed to open air until they were nearly full, which provided a great buffet for the rats. This may have been one of the reasons why most of the rats had disappeared from the hospital proper.

"Cook is very proud of herself. We shall leave her gloating for right now, but I think the rats have just moved on, their dead as dead as the people, and the survivors are looking for greener pastures."

James poured two healthy shots of antidote into glasses and interrupted her musings:

"Here, drink this, you need this to support your circulation, you are deathly pale, my dear."

She downed the fiery liquid with one swallow, gasping for breath.

"Wow, you are getting pretty good at that," he laughed. He admired her stamina but was not yet finished picking her brain. "Now tell me exactly how you know and foremost how it came to be that you are here with us plain people."

"Oh no, I am very sure I am plainer than all of you. I come from nothing. There are no doctors in my family which is pure working class and somewhat dysfunctional but not interesting enough to hold your attention for a single minute."

James finished his shot; put the glass down and grasping for both of her hands, peered into her frightened wide pupils. "It's time you tell!"

"There is nothing else. I have told you before that I have felt people's life strength through touch in my hands ever since I was a little girl going about with my Granny and Grandpa visiting their sick friends. Granny and her friend old Bella knew about herbs and teas and poultices. Most often their healthy intuition led them on the right path of healing. Yes, I would say Bella was a great healer. I do not know what she felt in her hands or in her heart. She just seemed to know instinctively the right thing to say and to do."

All these memories of Bella made Angelika sad, big hot tears started to gather blinding her and when she briefly closed her eyes the tears spilled over and down her pale cheeks.

"This is the second time you mentioned this Bella," James was now intrigued. "She must have been a very special friend that her memory is making you so sad. Has she been gone long? How about your Granny and Grandpa, have they all passed and left you alone? It must be the reason why you signed up for this work. Now it all makes sense to me, you poor thing." He was moved to pity for her assumed solitary state.

"But trust me; you will never be alone again. Together we will accomplish great things. Your intrinsic knowledge and my studies and station will make us a force to be reckoned with. We shall enlighten the world!"

Angelika could not believe her ears. How easily he had transferred tiny glimpses into her story into his particular time and space and made sense of it. She could have been off the hook, so to speak, but she wanted more. Much like Maria, who was trying to escape by giving up, all she wanted, was to be back (or forward?) towards reality; back to Bella and Granny, her girlhood, her studies but foremost her treasured innocence. Just as she had gathered her courage and was ready to tell all, he folded her into his arms, caressing her back, he whispered into her ears:

"When this nightmare is over, I want you to marry me! Promise, you marry me!"

Before she could respond, he kissed her hard and deeply, his hand sliding into her starched uniform. As much as Angelika wanted to stop it, she could not. He was so sincere; it felt so right at the moment, that she could not spoil it with her true or dreamy ghost story. She thought: 'The truth must wait. Perhaps all will sort itself out somehow without my interference. For how could I have appeared in the middle of this, if not for a dream?'

It had to be a dream, because she could not understand time-travel, no one could! So she kissed him back and helped him with those pesky little buttons and soon enough they found themselves entangled on his cot on his thin blanket and for a short time they forgot disease, fatigue and responsibility.

Once they had slipped back into their clothing, she reminded him of their duty:

"Elsa will surely miss me by now and we have to check on Maria!"

On wobly legs Angelika, helped along by James, ascended the steps to Matron's study. Maria was pale and still when they approached her cot. Cook had left a pitcher of tea and a bowl of broth at her bed-side. Both were untouched.

"Wake up, sleepy head," he called. James knelt down next to Maria, gently lifting her arms to probe her axillae for swollen glands. Dora had undressed her and clad her into one of her finely stitched night dresses, made from the thinnest muslin and finished with lace and embroidery. Once he freed her arms, they both stared at the shocking evidence of two immensely swollen glands under each armpit. They took in her otherwise flawless body, her swanlike neck perched on exquisitely muscled shoulders, her beautifully formed white breasts with very pink areolas. Angelika quickly covered her up; ashamed they may have seen too much, too much that was not offered consciously and willingly. Electric current ran all the way up and down her arms as she was redressing her. James read her expression and mumbled:

"Should we lance the buboes? I don't right know why I am asking you, it's the thing to do, there is nothing else. I know, you hate it and think it's no use, but we must try!"

Dora had overheard the last words as she entered the room:

"I'll assist, Dr. James, I can do it!" She quickly left the room but minutes later returned with Matron bearing basins, cotton-wool and the dreaded scalpel. Matron pulled a little bottle from her apron pocket:

"Mr. Paulus has prepared this especially for our Maria here. He assures me, that if properly administered, it will keep her unconscious and pain free throughout the procedure."

Angelika had wandered to the back of the room in an attempt to slide out. Unfortunately, Matron had sensed her dread and decided to put her to work.

"Here," she said, "take this dropper and fill it to the top. Now hold Maria's head to the side and gently try to drip a few drops on her tongue. Do it gently and slowly, so it will be absorbed from her tongue and she will not choke. Then you will feel her pulse and look at her pupils. Mr. Paulus said that the medicine contains opium and belladonna. Opium will make her sleep and take away pain, while belladonna widens the pupils, slows the heart and keeps her from choking while drying the mouth."

This was not exactly news to Angelika. Bella had told her about the dangers of poppy-seed tea and belladonna, the potion ancient ladies used to widen their pupils to pretend sexual arousal. She perched at the head of Maria's cot, holding her face to one side, she begged her to open her mouth to receive the medicine.

Maria was barely conscious at this time, but obediently opened her mouth, sensing that all was done to help her. After a few drops her eyes closed, her body became slack and relaxed. Dr. James could start the dreaded procedure of cutting and draining. They all donned black oil-coats and leather gloves. Dora held the basin and Matron kept Maria's shoulders firmly down on her cot, so she could not move. James felt her pulse and instructed Angelika to give her two more drops. The minute the sharp knife pierced the gland, Maria's head flopped from side to side and she started to moan. She gripped Angelika's hands and hung on for dear life. Soon it was over, the wounds washed with wine and dressed.

Dora had dressed Maria into one of the rough hospital shifts, since she thought that her own beautiful night dress was too nice to be fouled. Matron asked the girls who would like to stay and watch her until the medicine wore off. Dora volunteered eagerly:

"I'll stay with her!"

"So it's decided! You will take first watch, and later I will stay with her during the night!"

"That is very thoughtful of you, Matron, but it will not be necessary," Dora replied very seriously. "I will not leave her until she is well!" These last words hung in the air between all of them. It was the first hopeful thought they dared to have.

As Angelika was leaving the room with the offensive basin and the soiled dressing, she could not help but admire Dora, steadfast Dora, who had found her soul-mate in Maria. She turned around to take in that tableau of devotion; Dora sitting very close to Maria, holding her wrist and wiping the perspiration from her forehead with such an expression of concern, some would call love. In spite of the very painful procedure, Maria's face was relaxed and peaceful as if she could sense that she was lovingly and expertly cared for.

While Angelika was puzzled by Dora's behavior, Matron closed the door behind them with a look of pure understanding and said:

"Love comes in many forms and affects all of us in different ways. One needs to be open and accepting!" Angelika found this attitude admirable, because she had in her real time listened to many sordid and unpleasant accusations directed towards relationships of people of the same sex. She thought that she understood Dora, but Maria, who had been so critical and jealous of her time with James, she found confusing. She wondered if Maria felt like Dora and did not know herself or was ashamed of that emotion so that she could not or would not allow herself to succumb to those feelings. Perhaps because of her beauty, she had been pursued by many men and found them tedious and shallow.

'Be open and accepting; easier said, than done,' she thought. Besides, what is more disturbing; love and devotion among women friends or this sordid and illusionary alliance with the good Dr. James.'

Her head was throbbing from trying to sort out her feelings and the pressure of preserving her secret. Ever since Rose had accused her of witchcraft and conjuring up her illness and subsequent death, she felt terrified to divulge anymore of her story.

It was getting late. Everybody gathered once again in the dining hall. Ale was poured and drunk greedily by all. Cook had surprised them with baked chicken and potatoes. Matron could not get over the abundance:

"Chicken, how in the world did you manage that? It's wonderful! We are all getting pretty tired of fat back by now without appearing ungrateful of your efforts."

"Don't thank me, it's our good Mr. Paulus, he gave me a few bottles of antidote and I managed to trade them for these here chickens, beautiful fat ones this time, not those poor starved creatures we had before. No these ones have been well fed and now they will feed us. There is nothing better than a good fat roasted chicken to raise our spirits and the will to carry on!"

"Hear, hear!" James had raised his glass in agreement, "To our Maria, that she will beat this and return to us healthy and whole!"

"Praise God!" Matron said that this was their prayer tonight and for everyone to dig in. They all displayed a surprising appetite as the aroma of the roasted meat filled their nostrils. Angelika grabbed a wing.

'Mmm, chicken wings!' It had been so long since she tasted one of her favorite foods. She was amazed anew at how the smell of good food can raise the human spirit in spite of tremendous tragedies and thought:

'We truly are not much superior when our animal instincts take over, trumping sadness and loss by the arousal of our most primitive urges; food, drink and sex. Death and dying all around, but give us a chicken wing, well roasted, and life is bearable. We are a despicable lot when it comes down to that.'

Before retiring to their room the girls decided to check one more time on Maria, perhaps they could relieve Dora for a while. It was very quiet in the room. Dora had pushed a chair near the cot. Her head had sunk deeply onto her chest and she was snoring softly. In her lap the open Bible was teetering on the edge ready to slide to the floor. Elsa grabbed the Good Book. It was opened to the story of Jesus's healing of the young girl. The girl had already died, because he was summoned too late.

"I don't right remember what happened to the girl." Elsa looked anxiously at the pages.

"He raised her; told her to get up and to her mother to get her something to eat! What do you think Angelika? Can the same thing happen here?"

"First of all, Jesus is not present; all we can do is pray, but truthfully, I have little hope for her." The last words were whispered in case Maria was alert enough to overhear their conversation. Suddenly Dora awoke with a start:

"I am a great nurse, asleep on the job!" She looked contrite but so terribly tired that the girls felt sorry for her. Elsa took her hands and said firmly:

"You are deathly tired, my dear. Don't be upset. Maria is doing better, she is sleeping soundly and her fever is not worse."

"I think she looks a little better after the lancing," Angelika offered.

"Why don't I stay with her while you and Elsa get some sleep. I promise to call you, Dora, if anything changes."

Dora gratefully took the offer. She was physically and emotionally spent.

Angelika took Dora's place at Maria's bedside; picking up the Bible, she scanned the worn pages yellowed with age. The chapter's head lines were beautifully decorated with fancy scroll, the words written in an ancient script she recognized from Bella's herbal ledgers. The edges of the pages showed beautifully stylized paintings of flowers and birds flowing into each other gracefully. She thought them lovely and wondered how many hours it must have taken a person to write and paint this splendor. She thought that this particular version of the book was printed, but couldn't identify the age and origin since the first few pages were too worn and the script nearly faded. She took care to handle the pages gently, just like Bella and Granny had taught her. When she felt herself getting too tired, she laid down the Bible and before settling into a more comfortable position, reached over to feel Maria's pulse once more. Her color was still pale but not ashen and her pulse a steady drumbeat, she did not sense before. She wiped her forehead once more and dried her neck and chest where little rivulets of sweat collected in the hollows of her collar bone. The more she touched her, the more perplexed she became at the lack of vibration. There was nothing like the almost uncomfortable burning sensation she felt while they were lancing her glands.

"I think you are getting better against all odds," she whispered.

Maria opened her eyes and with all her might focused on Angelika's face above her. Angelika noticed her steady gaze and quickly pulled back as if she was caught at her thoughts.

Maria started to move her lips and was trying to speak, but her mouth and tongue were too dry. After Angelika gave her a few sips of tea, she was able to understand her softly whispered and hoarse words:

"Rose hated you; she thought you had made her sick. But I know better. You have no such powers; just a keen mind and perhaps visions."

"Oh, Maria I didn't fault Rose a bit. We got thrown together and she got ill so fast. I think she was already sick when she came to us."

"What do you know, Angelika? I think I have the right to know. I do not think you are a witch or a sorceress. It does not make sense; why would you expose yourself to this, if you could change shape, time and circumstance?" Maria's eyes were quite clear at this point. Her temperature was almost normal and her whispered words clear and kind. Angelika sat back in her chair, taking on the pose and face of complete capitulation; she dropped her hands to her sides and sighed. Looking straight into Maria's eyes, she told her story:

"I don't know why and how I can sense the life strength of the people I meet and minister too. I have had this curse or gift since I was a small child going around with my Granny visiting her sick friends. I have always known and don't know why I know when the end of a person's life is near. It was frightening until Bella, my Granny's old friend, told me, that it is a gift from God I need to cultivate and honor. I say a single prayer each time this feeling, these vibrations I feel in my arms comes to me. The prayer is simple. 'Dear God, please let me recognize only what comes from you, Amen.' First I thought it stupid, too simplistic, but it always worked, at least until now."

"What is different now; tell me, am I going to die?"

"Two hours ago I was sure that you would. My arms nearly jumped from my body when I was holding you down for the lancing."

"Curiously I felt none of that." Maria felt around her axillae and groins, her hands patting the thick cotton wool bandages Dora refreshed before leaving.

"That was due to Mr. Paulus's potion we dripped down your throat that gave you sound sleep. I was really worried that we were giving you too much of a good thing. It's probably wearing off by now and you must be in a great deal of pain!

"No, just a little pain, but you did not answer my question!"

"To be honest Maria, I am confused. I feel almost nothing, as if you have never taken ill at all. It is really not crazy. James believes that lancing drops the fever and some get better. I think you belong to those."

"That sounds too good to be true, but it's not the whole story, is it?" Maria pushed herself up higher on her pallet in order to study Angelika's expression:

"How do you know about tiny fleas attacking rats, and about even tinier animals one cannot see, which can make us ill? How do you know about the heart and the pulse and hot water coming from pipes and how is it possible that you have never been to a privy? I saw how candlelight makes you squint and how you could not make a simple little fire to heat a cup of water for tea. There are so many other things you could not do and there is even more you could not or would not explain to us." Maria was now breathless from her long and emotional speech. She lay back on her pillow and closed her eyes in weakness, waiting for Angelika to explain herself.

"Promise me, that you will not tell a soul, even if you don't believe me, for I cannot explain it. Have you ever heard of time-travel? Your mind plays tricks and suddenly you find yourself in a different time and place."

"You mean a dream-like state?"

"Yes, it is much like a dream, except you don't wake up. Each passing day becomes more fantastic than the one before and reality shifts. For the first twenty-four hours all I did was pinch my face and my arms to force myself to wake up but to no avail. I was here with you and the others, caught in this nightmare and I don't know why."

Maria's eyes got bigger and bigger, for she could not believe her ears. "That explains a lot, you are not from here!"

"I am not," Angelika admitted tearfully. "After experiencing a great tragedy, I fell asleep in Bella's rocking chair, after she gave me some tea to drink to calm me down. When I woke up, I sat in that old chair in this ward, where the good Dr. James found me and introduced me to you all."

Maria's hand reached over to grasp Angelika's as to make sure that she was really made of flesh and blood. So convinced; she petted her hand and whispered:

"Is it your time to go back?"

"Not back, but forward. My time is 1967. We have electricity, cars and television, tall buildings and elevators, real hospitals, drugs and x-rays and...." She broke down and covered her face with her hands and started to sob uncontrollably, while Maria stared at her, this strange creature who seemed to babble nonsense. After a few seconds, she could not help but ask:

"What's an elevator?" Angelika stopped crying, seeing Maria's baffled expression, she started to grin. Wiping her eyes, she explained:

"We have very tall buildings one hundred stories high with too many steps to climb, so you step into a little electric booth, push the button and you get powered up and down depending on which button is pushed. It's all done with power that comes from a motor, which moves with a spark. I am sorry, I don't know exactly how, but it works unless there is a power failure, then we get candles and the lucky ones have a fireplace to burn wood for heat."

"Mr. Paulus said, the body makes sparks which move the heart, like when you rub wood together or when you are lucky enough to find the hard stone called flint. That must be what you feel, Angelika, sparks from the heart."

The more Angelika thought about Maria's simplistic explanation, the more sense it made. This last conversation exhausted Maria. She closed her eyes and drifted off to sleep. Angelika could not wait to give Dora the good news.

'Maria will live. I am quite sure this time.'

Right now she was too tired to get up, pushing herself as deeply into the easy chair as she could, she pulled a rug over her shoulders and went to sleep too. Earlier she had opened a window; a warm breeze lifted the muslin curtains and caressed both girls, the tall beautiful one, breathing deeply the even sighs of the recovering body, and the other so different one, with the pinched and narrow wheeze of the exhausted. That's how Dora found them, when she got up from her rest to be at Maria's side.

While Maria's cheeks had lost their pallor and she was breathing deeply and evenly the healing sleep of recovery, Angelika had sunk down in her chair and her breath came raspy and raggedly from her mouth. Dora felt her forehead and was shocked to find it hot and damp. On further examination, she found her pulse weak and haltingly with longer pauses than normal.

"Angelika, wake up, you must lie down, I am here to relieve you!" She opened her eyes slowly, barely able to focus and croaked:

"I think, I got it, but Maria is saved!"

"What nonsense you speak, my dear; it's exhaustion, nothing else!" Her shaky voice betrayed her when she continued:

"I will get James for you right now!"

"No fuss please, let him sleep. He can see me tomorrow."

"It's tomorrow, silly!" With that she ran down the passage to James's office. Banging like a maniac at the door, she screamed:

"Get up; it's Angelika, hurry!"

James opened the door. Standing in his long underwear, rubbing his red rimmed eyes, he tried to understand:

"What's with Angelika?"

"She is sick, James, you have to come and get her. She fell asleep in Maria's room where she held watch all night."

James quickly jumped into his trousers, forgetting his shirt; he followed Dora to Matron's study. The minute he laid eyes on Angelika, he knew that Dora was right. Her face was red hot and she was barely conscious. He scooped her up in his arms, running down the hall with her, he laid her on his cot and sank to his knees beside her. Dora followed him and standing in the doorway, she was almost embarrassed witnessing this scene of utter devotion and despair.

"Let me get her undressed," she offered.

"No, just leave, I will take care of her, just get out!" James screamed almost angrily.

Dora's eyes filled with tears, her hand clamped over her mouth, afraid to make a sound, she withdrew and closed the door behind her.

James bent over Angelika's limp body lying on his cot. With shaking hands he removed the dress with the starched collar and cuffs, her apron and her stockings and covered her with a thin cotton blanket. His hands working gently but deftly, he did not miss the telltale signs of plague, slightly swollen glands under her arms and groins. She winced in her feverish state when he palpated the swellings. Then he bathed her body with cool wine and spooned some between her cracked lips which she swallowed greedily. After he wet her lips and throat in such a manner, she opened her eyes, resting on his face, she whispered:

"It's a life for a life! Maria will live and I will go back. It is the only way. Don't try to change it or stop it. I must go back to my real...." The last words were spoken so softly, that he could not understand them, nor understand the meaning.

"You are not going anywhere, my darling. Not if I can help it. I love you and I want you with me forever, can you hear me?"

She did not, for she had slipped into that blessed state, that only a very high fever can achieve, the state of deep oblivion. Later Matron, Elsa and Dora came to take turns at her bedside. James only left her long enough to take care of the other patients, who by now were almost all on the mend. He could not wipe Angelika's last words from his memory.

'A life for a life. What crap!' he thought. 'She must pull through. Her glands never got bigger, lancing was not an option. He remembered how she hated it. Well at least she is spared that what she abhorred the most.'

Unfortunately her fever never responded to any treatment. It remained high and left her blessedly semiconscious. After twenty-four hours Maria was well enough to walk to Angelika's side with Dora's help. Seated at her bedside, she took her hand and whispered into her ear:

"I understand, soon you will be home!"

As if Angelika sensed Maria's nearness, she opened her eyes one last time, looking around at the faces of her dear friends, she said with considerable strength:

"I see, I know we will meet again," and breathed her last.

Chapter 11

A Life for a Life

Angelika felt herself fall. There was nothing to hold onto. She was falling down, down, down into darkness. She became liquid, like water pouring from a pipe into a bottomless pit. No conscious or subconscious thought, no fright or anxiety accompanied her exit. It was a simple winding down, an easy sailing through time and space without boundaries, until the movement stopped and she was once again solid. Just as effortlessly as her mind had adjusted to its ethereal quality, she was able to concentrate her energies once again on being earthbound.

She simply opened her eyes and stared into the familiar but frightened grey irises of Bella, who had fallen on her knees in front of the rocking chair, grasping Angelika's shoulders and was giving her the stern command to wake up!

"Wake up, you silly little girl, it has been hours, everyone will be so worried!" Once she saw her eyelids flutter and then open to a wide unfocused stare, she knew Angelika had returned from somewhere far away. She had already checked and rechecked the herbal mixture; she used to prepare the tea, which was usually so helpful in creating relaxation during times of severe stress. Mumbling to herself, she repeated:

"Two parts lemon balm, two parts chamomile, two parts valerian, one part St.-John's-wort and one part mint."

Bella was dancing around her little hut repeating to herself this recipe she had prepared so often in the past. She pulled most of her dried herb stocks from their hooks, crunching them between her discolored thumb and forefinger to emit their fragrance, thereby convincing herself that she had not made a mistake. Still mumbling she climbed her ladder to the highest shelf, which held the jars of more dangerous herbs and powders, such as hemlock, poppy-seed and arsenic. People think they are poisons, which they are, but in minute and proper amounts they are extremely potent healers. 'Am I getting too old?' she wondered. She was almost one hundred.

'Perhaps I got confused and mixed the poppy-seed with the lemon-balm. No, I am sure I did not. But why this deep sleep? Perhaps she was in a suggestive state? Perhaps I should not have added St. John's-wort.'

Poor Bella, she was clearly in a state of extreme agitation as she was watching Angelika slip into a deep sleep, but always breathing deeply and evenly. She observed her carefully; listening to her ranting and raving, picking up names here and there. Maria, Rose, Elsa, Dora seemed to be prevalent. James she called out repeatedly. Bella did not know all of Angelika's friends, but could not recall her ever mentioning those names. She lived through a few anxious hours, pacing about her hut and wondering what was happening to the poor girl whose features eventually relaxed, the ranting stopped and she slowly surfaced to her surroundings.

"Open your eyes, my dear girl!" was Bella's stern command.

Angelika listened and the minute she recognized dear old Bella kneeling in front of her and she felt the rocking chair give slightly under her weight, she smiled and leaning forward hugged that old frail woman so hard that they nearly both toppled over.

"Oh, my God Bella, you will never believe where I have been!"

"You have been right here in my chair the whole time giving me a fright." Bella looked positively puzzled.

"And who is Maria, Elsa, Dora, and... Rose?" Angelika added.

"Yes Rose, who are they?"

"It's a long story, dear, dear Bella. Soon I will tell you the entire thing, but right now I have to run. I must get home, Granny will be so worried. How long have I slept?"

"Nearly eight hours," said Bella. "You must have really been exhausted." Angelika jumped up, feeling slightly dizzy, she held on to the windowsill. "It's dark outside!" In jumping up she disturbed the cat that was sleeping next to the stove and seeing his opportunity leapt up to finally reclaim his rightful spot on the rocking chair.

"I will go with you and explain to your family why you have been gone so long."

"But how about your cataracts? You don't see well at night!"

"That is true my dear, but I don't have to see in the woods, they are my home. I know every tree and stone, shadows will guide me home." This was one of Bella's favorite phrases, one that always puzzled Angelika.

It had gotten much colder outside. Angelika wrapped herself in one of Bella's hand-knitted sweaters and Bella took her large square woolen wrap. Together they set out towards home. As they approached the house, they saw a crowd of people gathered outside. Angelika recognized some neighbors and friends from school. They turned around and once they recognized her in the mist, someone shouted:

"There she is!" It was Grandpa's idea to form a search party. He knew how upset Angelika had been earlier, when she stormed out of the house without a coat, gloves and a hat in the middle of winter. Since the girl's drowning, the whole town was in an uproar. They had checked the town, the river and the park but totally forgot about Bella. Since Bella's move from the neighborhood to the edge of the forest, she had also moved from their minds. Most were not unhappy to see her leave, since she evoked in them a sense of awe mixed with fear, causing discomfort mingled with guilt.

Granny could not believe her eyes and clasped Angelika into her arms like she never wanted to let her go. Once Grandpa realized the drama was resolved, he grumbled something under his breath that sounded like:

"There is nothing but trouble with women regardless of their age."

Then he grabbed Angelika from behind, so the three of them, including Bella and Granny formed a human wreath, squeezing her so tight, that she could hardly draw a breath inside the huddle.

It was over for Grandpa. "Enough excitement for one day," he mumbled and quickly withdrew into his tailor shop, thinking about this little bottle of vodka hidden in the third drawer of his sewing machine, which was his prescription for such turmoil. Meanwhile Granny invited Bella in for a cup of strong coffee:

"We all need something," she said.

They walked the few steps to Granny's kitchen where she quickly put on the kettle. The minute that first splash of boiling water soaked the freshly ground beans, the aroma was so lovely and comforting to Angelika, that she had to hold back tears.

"Oh how I missed that aroma, where I was, all they had was chicory and tea."

Bella tried to catch Granny's eye who was still trying to take this in. "And where might that have been," she asked.

"I know now that it was a dream, but so terribly real that I have a hard time trying to forget it."

"Let's have a cup and then you can tell us all about this terrible dream." Granny seeing the serious and almost panicky expression in her eyes was trying to lighten the mood.

"Oh, how good this tastes! I have had a heavy head and a pounding ache over my eyes from that tea and all that ale."

"You had ale?" Granny asked.

"Ale and some kind of liquor, they called Arrak. I wonder if there is such a drink. It tasted terrible but Mr. Paulus said that it was an antidote, so we all drank as much as we could."

"Who in the world is Mr. Paulus, anybody we know?" Granny could not get over the details Angelika seemed to remember from her dream.

"Mr. Paulus was the apothecary and there were Dr. James and Matron, cook, Elsa, Maria, Dora, Rose and many others I cannot quite remember. Oh yeah, and of course all the sick; Minnie, Marie, her children and..." her eyes were wide with fright and her pale face shone with little beads of perspiration as if it was difficult and painful to remember.

Granny was getting more and more perplexed, but Bella calmed them down by reassuring them of the fact that this most likely was a very vivid nightmare that Angelika will forget in time and get on with her life as before. Angelika stared into her cup:

"I am glad this is not tea and we don't have to read the tea leaves. That gave me the creeps each time, especially when it all seemed to come true."

"Reading tea leaves, eh," Bella cackled. "If I had known you had interest in that, I could have taught you a thing or two." Somehow Bella found this amusing until Granny interfered:

"Enough! My dear friend, you know how I feel about those things, fortunetelling and witchery. As far as I am concerned we are all in God's hands, and if we believe, he will not steer us wrong or desert us in our time of need, there is no need for tea leaves, playing cards or gypsies."

"You are absolutely right, Granny, because I feel that my prayers saved me and brought me back to you."

"But my dear child," cried Bella, "you were never gone. I watched you sleep in my rocking chair the whole time. I grant, it was not a quiet sleep; you stirred and moaned at times, but you were never physically away from me."

Angelika's pallor, somewhat diminished after the second cup of strong coffee, turned into rosy cheeks and the feverish frightened look in her eyes had calmed enough, that she was able to spill her whole dream. She told them about plague with its buboes, the horrible lancing, the stiff uniform with its scratchy starched collars and cuffs that left raw itchy marks on her neck and arms and about death and dying she experienced in those ancient wards.

"Oh Bella," she said, "they said it was 1679. It was a terrible time for people. They had hardly anything in their hospital. They washed wounds with vinegar and wine. There were no stethoscopes or a regular laboratory. The doctor leaned his ear directly against the chest of the sick person to listen to his lungs. There was so much suffering that it was unbearable. They thought plague came from the air and the doctors wore oil-cloth coats and strange birdlike helmets, which they stuffed with some type of strong smelling herb, thinking that it would kill the disease in the air before it reached their noses. It was all so sad and I wanted to help, but I did not know how. I was afraid, that they might not believe me. I was a coward, Granny!" With that she broke down again and started to sob as if her heart was breaking.

"But why were you so afraid?" Bella thought that Angelika needed to get as much of her story off her chest, as to heal her soul from this nightmare.

"I was afraid that they might think me a witch or some kind of sorceress with powers they could not understand. I was afraid they would throw me in the loony bin or worse burn me at the stake for heresy. After all it was 1679."

"I knew you read way too much child," Granny was shaking her head, but sensing that her distress was much too real, not like the aftermath of a nightmare, when one wakes up and is able to shake off the dread, blaming a full stomach or an overwrought mind. So she suggested that they stop talking about it for right now, since it seemed to upset her more. She knew that a trauma relived is just as distressing to the mind as the initial event. By now it was getting very late and Bella got up, wrapping her woolen shawl around her person tightly she sighed:

"It's time for me to go home, you are in good hands my dear girl and whenever you ready we will sort all this out together. By the way; did you say Arrak?"

Angelika was nodding her head.

"I have a bottle like that on my shelf. I use it to prepare certain herbs. It is a type of rum and very strong. It will burn your throat when taken undiluted. Perhaps you saw it at one time or another and wondered about it."

Bella then slowly pulled herself up from the chair, grabbed her walking stick heading for the door with the considerable limp she had for some time now. Once she was gone, Granny said:

"I don't know about Bella, she sure is getting on in years, close to a hundred, I say. Now let me make you something to eat, you were too upset earlier."

She busied herself in their tiny kitchen, slicing bread and putting butter, cheese and sausage on a plate. "We shall have a cold supper, call your Grandpa!"

"Please no ale or tea," cried Angelika, "I have had enough of that during my last three days."

Granny could not get over the idea that Angelika was convinced she had missed three whole days. However she was wise enough to let the story rest for the moment, knowing that Angelika would come around to supply them with a better understanding of this all too vivid nightmare she had endured. While Granny set the table; humming a little church tune under her breath, Angelika went up to her room to change her clothes and to freshen up. Hot water from the spigot ran over her hands.

'I'll never take this for granted again, as long as I live. I'll never be able to tell them the rest of my story. Granny would not understand about James. In time I will also think about it as a dream, the nightmare everybody seems to think I had. I wonder if Bella knows about time-travel. How could it have been a dream, when I can still feel his hands on my body, have his scent in my nose and hear his voice in my head? (You cannot leave me, I love you!) Who dreams like this? Only a mad person!'

There were too many unanswered questions making her head spin. Her room was unchanged, her bed was made and her school books packed away for good. She sat down on her bed, slipping off her shoes and socks, her jeans and shirt, even her underpants and bra. Once she laid back on her bed, feeling the smoothness of the sheets under her, so different from the rough spun cotton of the 17th century. Balling her underwear together and burying her nose in its soft folds, she was sure without a doubt, that she recognized the faint odor of camphor and alcohol mixed with the scent of her own sweat and something else she could only identify as him. Tears sprung to her eyes and the sheer terror of going mad cramped her chest and tightened her solar plexus. It was Granny's voice that brought her back to reality:

"Dinner, Angelika hurry up!"

She quickly slipped into her night gown and robe and hurried downstairs.

"I see you have made yourself comfortable," said Grandpa, who did not relish seeing people in loungewear at the dinner table.

"I am sorry Grandpa, I am wearing my robe. I just had to get rid of my clothes; they were really dirty after three days."

Grandpa's eyebrows shot up at the mentioning of three days, but Granny's stern look and swift kick to his chins under the table silenced the question that was on his tongue.

Angelika did not realize how hungry she was, looking at the smoked sausages and Swiss cheese; taking a big hunk of brown bread, she layered it with meat and cheese, topping it off with spicy mustard, thick slices of red onion, fresh juicy tomatoes and a sprinkling of black pepper.

"May I have a glass of beer?" she asked Granny, who nodded and poured her a healthy measure from Grandpa's bottle. His eyebrows shot up again, but another kick under the table stemming from Granny's' sturdy legs and leather shoes stopped him again. Supper was consumed in silence, which suited Angelika just fine. Granny did not want to stir her up and Grandpa was nursing two bruised chins and kept his mouth shut. Since nobody was making conversation and he was deprived of such, he picked up the day's paper that he had not been able to read because of the earlier excitement of the search. There was a little note on the front page. He read it quietly to himself:

'Drowned girl raises questions of ice skating safety on frozen river!' Then he continued out loud:

"The burial of the girl is tomorrow; all school classes and teachers will attend the ceremony.

I guess that includes you!"

Angelika who just taken a bite from her sandwich looked stunned.

"We will all go," said Granny, "it's the least we can do for the family."

Angelika was trying to digest the information Grandpa had read. She had completely forgotten what had put her in Bella's rocking chair in the first place. She looked up and somehow lost her appetite.

"I did not know her very well. I only talked to her a couple of times. The last time we talked; we stood on the bridge watching the skaters having fun below, and when she took my hand, I knew without a doubt that something was going to happen to her. I did not know when and where and how. When the news came that she had drowned by slipping under the ice, my brain just went haywire. That's why I ran to Bella, because I knew, she would understand."

"I am so sorry, child. I also understand what this had done to you. Tomorrow we will go to the funeral and pay our respects. It may put your mind to rest."

Angelika was grateful for Granny's calming words, while Grandpa, shoving the last bit of bread into his mouth, got up from the table immediately which was not his routine, and mumbled under his breath:

"Women-folk with their feelings and intuitions, pure nonsense if you ask me."

"Well, nobody is asking!" Granny looked somewhat perturbed, for she had heard every word. Grandpa got up, rubbing his sore chins, mumbling something else while trying to flee the scene as fast as possible while Granny and Angelika looked at each other conspiringly and smiled.

Chapter 12

Earning that Life

School was over for Angelika, her life's path set. She decided to go to nursing school. Her choices were limited. She could not imagine sitting in an office or a bank all day pushing paper and pencil or working in a shop. Since there was no money available for her to go to the university to study medicine or pharmacy, her true love, she decided that nursing school was her only option. It was free, requiring no money up front but relied heavily on her ability to labor in the hospital while studying the required curriculum at the hospital affiliated nursing school.

It was a beautiful summer day, sunny and warm, when she packed her little wicker basket and set out to board the train taking her to her destination in a neighboring town about one hour away from home. She had had a couple more good cries and talks with Bella where they rehashed the dream or as Bella called it the 'day-scare'. Angelika remembered every detail of her strange experience and shared most of it with Bella. To herself she kept all that involved James. It remained a mystery, for no matter how real her encounter with him felt; she recognized the impossibility of it. However, each time she recalled their conversation, each word and each touch, made it more difficult for her to return to reality. The boys interested in her now seemed silly, their conversations immature and their clumsy hands unbearable. Soon they thought her stuck up and found her attitude boring at best. When they distanced themselves and took a few friends with them, Angelika felt more relief than abandonment. She most often sought a quiet place in the woods, where she listened to the song of birds and the twitter of insects.

"You must forget your dream," said Granny. "Go out with your young friends and have a good time!"

It was sound advice but seemed impossible. Often at night she would wake up with the smell of death in her nostrils and the screams of the suffering in her ears. Bathed in sweat and with her heart pounding in her chest, she would sit up, taking in deep gulps of air and force herself back to awareness. She questioned Bella frequently why this continued to happen to her and why she could not forget. Bella, who still went over the tea mixture in her mind, thinking that it might have caused a hallucigenic episode with flashbacks, was cautious with her answer. One evening with the fire blazing in the stove and the cat peacefully on his favorite chair, Bella started with a new approach to alleviate Angelika's nightmares.

"Perhaps you don't want to forget," she said. "Perhaps, something happened that caused you to change from the person you were before and perhaps, it was wonderful."

Bella leaned forward; her veiled grey-green eyes sparkling in the fire light had an eerie almost hypnotic effect on Angelika, who was rocking gently with her eyes closed, listening to Bella's soft voice like a familiar soothing litany. Once she caught the intended meaning, she stopped rocking and tried to catch Bella's eyes with an attempt to stare her down. It never worked.

"You are a witch!" she finally hissed. "The people are right, you have bewitched me and to answer your insinuation; No, I did not change, nothing happened and I do want to forget all and everything I saw in that dream!"

The vehemence with which she shouted the last two sentences, proved Bella's suspicions. "Calm down," she crooned. "You are not bewitched, just sensitive for you know that I have touched a nerve."

"I just cannot talk about it! It's too sad, people died, you know."

"People always die, my dear; we are here for a little while, some shorter, some longer and then we are gone, gone into the atmosphere, to the spirit-world where nothing ever dies. They are all around us, every one of your spirit people, especially Rose. I believe she is the one not letting you rest!"

Angelika was really agitated now, jumping out of her chair, she cried:

"Can you see Rose?"

"No, not directly, but you mentioned her name more than anybody else."

"Because she frightened me more than the others. She thought I was the enemy and caused her illness. She called me a witch."

"Is that not what you are accusing me of now?" Bella said quietly.

"Oh, I am sorry, I did not mean it. I don't even know where that came from. Of course you are not a witch, just wise, but you found me out, which made me angry. It is not just Rose; there is another I cannot forget. His name is James and we got to be very close."

"You are a grown woman and this kind of phantasy is normal."

"But Bella, the problem is; I don't think it's a phantasy. He was real and I can't get him out of my head, my mind and most importantly my senses."

"Perhaps it is a premonition, a sign of what is yet to come," Bella said with a smile.

"I hope you are right, because he is the one I want."

This candid conversation with her trusted friend seemed to help. Angelika's nightmares became less bothersome and soon a distant memory and she was able to get on with her life.

The life of a student nurse and the study of man became all consuming. For now she was so busy, she almost forgot her previous experience with the sick. She shared a room with three other girls her age and they became fast friends. Her introduction to the modern hospital world was much like what she had seen as a young girl hiding under Granny's bed. Only everything had improved over the years. There were more medications and procedures. She had not realized the amount of paperwork that needed to be kept up on each individual patient. Also the huge volumes of nursing books and intense evening studies under the most dedicated doctors left little time to worry about nightmares and lost friends.

Her favorite time was spent on the individual hospital units in direct contact with her patients. She was quick and thought of as intuitive when it came to their care. Her uniform was simple; a white dress without apron, a jaunty little starched folded cap and comfortable shoes. No starched collars and cuffs chafed her arms and neck and even though she had to pin up her hair, the cap was light in comparison with the full weighty contraption in her dream. There were ward-sisters in charge and while some were mean and bossy, most had their own full lives with husbands and children. She was fascinated with the study of the human body. Microbiology, the study of bacteria and viruses opened her eyes to the marvels of modern medicine. 'Oh what I would have given to have that knowledge in my dream,' she often thought and had to remind herself that it made no difference for it was a dream. What remained her constant companion was her gift of intuition. Going about the business of healing and handling the sick entrusted to her care still made her anxious. More often than she liked, did she feel vibrations in her arms which warned her of the patients' demise. If they were very old or very ill it was expected, but if the person was young and recovering from a minor illness or surgery, she often panicked, summoning the attending physician to plead the patient's case. While her concern was often written off as the over anxious worrying of an inexperienced student nurse, the staff learned soon enough to take her warnings seriously. It pleased her to use her gift, for often a disastrous outcome was averted.

Patients came and went and their stories blended into one another weaving a solid mesh of experience and confidence. She learned much and after three years felt comfortable enough to rely on her own judgments. Her co-workers and physicians learned to listen to her and appreciate her concerns. She stopped fretting about her feelings, but accepted them, asking God to only let her know that which came from him. For the most part this seemed to ease her apprehension.

Days and nights spent on various hospital floors were always busy and while most stories of the human condition played out in those wards and operating theaters were routine and lumped together, a few stuck out because of their extraordinary sadness or circumstance.

One of those is the story of Anne, a young woman diagnosed with breast cancer. One night while Angelika was working the night shift, Anne became very distraught, ringing the bell:

"Can you give me a sleeping pill?" she asked.

Angelika replied, "Let me see what the doctor ordered. You have already had one and your pain medication."

"Oh blast that doctor! Just give me all I can have, so I can finally forget."

At this point Anne was sure that she was losing her battle with breast cancer. She had had surgery, chemotherapy and radiation, but her cancer had erupted underneath of her mastectomy scar and had spread in large ugly and painful sores across her chest and back. Her hair was gone and her voice had deepened to a soft tenor from hormone therapy which she received as a last and experimental resort. Angelika knew that she had the rare inflammatory type of breast cancer which responds poorly to treatment. She was also sure of Anne's impending death. After checking on her other patients, she returned to Anne's room, which was private and located in the privileged area of the ward. Anne was the wife of a prominent physician in town. She had two children, a boy five and a girl three years old.

"I called the doctor for you, Anne, because I can't give you any more medication on my own, I am sorry!" Angelika moved a chair closer to Anne's bed and sat down. "He will call me back or stop in shortly."

Anne was nodding her head, her face once beautiful, was ravished with acne from the testosterone shots, and her eyes were red from crying. Angelika took her hand, little electric shocks moved up her forearms and tingled in her hands and she knew without a doubt that Anne's days of suffering were numbered.

"You are a funny little nurse," Anne croaked, "Not much to you but you seem wise beyond your years. Let me tell you a story."

With that Anne opened her heart and out came one of the saddest confessions of shame and guilt that Angelika had witnessed in her career so far. After taking a few sips of water to wet her dry lips and throat, Anne started with the hoarse whisper that had become her voice:

"My husband and I were students together at a famous university. We were in love. Both of our parents were rich and we had a privileged childhood. His father is a famous surgeon and my family owns the pharmaceutical company in town, producing a well-known and highly sought after drug. We had the world by the ass." she smiled, then laughed a laugh which turned into coughing. Exhausted she laid back onto her pillow and continued:

"He studied medicine and I pharmacy. Working side by side in the laboratory for long hours had started our friendship. After two years we became lovers and married. It was the most beautiful and ostentatious wedding our community had seen in years."

Her lusterless eyes glowed with the memory.

"My dress was silver white and I had eight bridesmaids. Over five hundred people were invited, so nearly the whole town celebrated with us. We moved immediately into our own home which was remodeled and newly furnished. We were the luckiest people in the world with love, commitment and all the worldly goods money could buy."

She leaned back again exhausted and took another drink from the glass Angelika held to her lips.

"We had one more year to study before he could start his residency and I could begin my work as a chemist in my father's company. Have you met my husband?" she asked suddenly.

"No, I have not had the pleasure."

"Oh, you must see him; he is so gorgeous! Even when he walked down the aisle, I could not believe that he married me. Every time I saw him walking towards me, in a restaurant or at work, I was always stunned anew that he picked me. That feeling never left me."

She paused again, clearly evaluating Angelika's reaction. But Angelika did not move a muscle; she only listened intently, never letting go of her hand.

"It was during that third year, when evil entered our life. My periods were never regular so I relied on regular precautions in order not to get pregnant before we were finished with our studies. I had missed a couple of periods before, so I was not immediately concerned, when it fell out for several months. I ignored the tell-tale signs of swollen breasts and nausea, because I knew how upset he would be about having a baby at this time. You see up til now, the fairytale romance, wedding and, foremost, his career had happened as scheduled. When my symptoms could no longer be denied, I told him. We were married and financially secure, so his reaction came as a total surprise. It all came down to the easy going life style and the sexy girl he did not want to give up. He was not ready to accept me as a wife and mother. And I..., I was too afraid to lose him, this beautiful man with his easy smile and endearing way that I agreed to the abortion. Since it was illegal and I was too far along; a friend of my husband performed the deed after- hours in his surgery."

At this point her voice was so low and her expression so pained, that Angelika feared for her life:

"Please don't exert yourself; this is too painful for you to bring all this up."

"But I must, you see, that night my husband, the third year medical student, and his friend murdered our son with my complicacy. The procedure was not easy; I was much further along than either of us suspected. Since they were afraid to put me to sleep, I was awake and aware of everything. I don't remember the pain, there had to have been pain, but I will never forget his cry, when he was forced from my womb. He cried only once and I saw his little stick arms flailing in the air between my legs and then it was quiet. He was murdered and discarded like a rotten chicken into a bin with other medical waste to be burned the following day. And this is how I let evil into our lives. I stayed in bed for three days, unable to eat or sleep, just stared into space. 'You must eat, get back to normal!' advised my husband, 'there will be other children when the time is right!' No damage had been done, was his friends assessment of my condition. Oh how we fooled ourselves into believing this. Life went on as planned. I finished my studies with honors and my husband started his residency. Two years later he thought it the right time to start a family, to have that wanted child. Since my depression in spite of medication never left me completely, I thought it might be a good idea as well. My son was born strong and healthy, but I could not fully see him; all I saw were two red stick arms flailing between my legs and hear that small cry for help. I tried to be a good mother and dutifully had a second child, my daughter now three years old. I continued working part time as a chemist and took care of my children; running from appointment to appointment kept my body and mind racing, so I did not have to think. Until my diagnosis about a year ago this approach seemed to work. My husband refused to broach any subject concerning the loss of our first son. That wound remained, at least for me, wide open much like the lesions I have developed on my chest and back. I know now, that nothing can ever wipe out that sin, so healing is impossible."

Anne's attending doctor had entered the room quietly during the last part of her tale. He took her hand and very softly said:

"That is untrue; you can make it better, perhaps there is no cure, but you have suffered more than most with this disease. It has pruned you of all for that next stage. I am sure of it."

Angelika was surprised at this doctor's soothing words, for he usually did not get too involved with his patient's state of mind.

"So you think I have been punished enough?" she added.

"When I die and meet my murdered son, how can I ever explain my actions?" Taking a deep ragged breath, her eyes spilling over with tears, as she continued:

"Perhaps he will recognize me, because my living children don't. They refuse to visit me; my little girl cried in fear when I tried to hug her. You see, everything about me has changed, my appearance, even my voice frightens them. My little boy asked to have his mommy back, not that ugly old man in the bed."

Both Angelika and the doctor were stunned at that last outburst, at the rawness of this grief which seemed to drain her of all strength. Angelika was allowed to administer another shot for pain and comfort to help Anne sleep and foremost forget for the moment. Just before Angelika was leaving the room, Anne opened her eyes once more and mumbled:

"Promise you won't tell a soul of what you heard. I have never talked about this to anybody."

"I promise!" Angelika said and took her cold hand again. "Now try and get some sleep, let the medicine work!"

It was one of the sadder stories Angelika had heard and one of the sadder deaths she had to witness.

Every day presented with new challenges. Patients came and went; most got better, some did not; and many died, in spite of medical advances, in her care. She always felt it a special privilege to witness these most important human events; births and deaths, first hand. While the maternity wards brought endless joy and only occasional heartache and disappointment, the medical units often let her experience the passing of a human soul from the body into the universe unknown. After witnessing this, she was absolutely certain, that it is only the body that dies. It is the soul that passes from one reality to the next. This spark, which is there one minute, illuminating the eyes and psyche of a human body, and gone the next leaving an empty shell.

It was the nurse's job to prepare the body to be viewed by the family immediately after death and then to be taken to the morgue.

Death did not frighten her. Even as a child she had made the rounds with Granny often enough to recognize the signs of a person's demise. Always aware of her gift, she learned to use it as a true advocate for her patients while there was still hope.

When it was her turn to prepare the body, she generally said a prayer for the departed soul. She washed their faces, closed their eyes and pulled out the now unnecessary IV-lines and tubes. She then gently cleaned them from all medical interventions they may have suffered. She did not mind this work. While her hands were busy she let her mind wander.

'I wonder what kind of a person he was.' A finely chiseled face and a prominent chin pointed to a strong gene pool, perhaps of genteel lineage. A powerful build and callused hands with large knuckles and stained nails would be the hands of a man who made his living working the fields or in the mines, while a tender skinned very thin body may have enjoyed a more pampered lifestyle. A fat person told of a love for food and drink and a sedentary life.

"I wash their limbs and brush their hair while I pray. It is most often the last time their bodies would be touched in this intimate yet caring way here on earth. I don't mind," she used to say, "at least they don't complain, for they feel no pain. It is the last service we are privileged to give."

Once the family said their good-byes and had their cry, the body was transferred to the hospital morgue. This was the only part of this particular duty she hated; the finality of the bagged body on the tray being pushed roughly into the cooler drawer. The loud metal-on-metal clank as the door was locked into place did not seem natural or refined. It was an abrupt end of the journey for the person in her care.

Once in the middle of the night, shortly before her final exam, all the students were summoned to the maternity ward. Most had had their turn in the delivery room and had seen their share of healthy babies born. If they were underweight or had special problems which this hospital could not handle, since it was not equipped with a neo-natal intensive care unit, the infants had to be transferred to the university hospital about an hour's drive away. Angelika always hated the tense ride in the ambulance, hoping to deliver the child safely.

This time it was different! A baby had been born nearly to term. Unfortunately it was extremely small, about two pounds and it had remained in the developmental stage of a fish according to a rare and complex genetic defect. It lacked a neck and where arms and legs would have formed, it had little raised nubs reminiscent of a fish's fin. The mouth was large, opening and closing with little gasps and the eyes were hidden by sealed eyelids. It was an astonishing sight. The doctors and the midwife in charge thought it educational for all of the students to witness this, because of its rarity. Angelika was appalled at the clinical rudeness. While she never actually saw the fetus breathe, she was sorry for the poor mother, who must have felt helpless and exposed in her grief, when curious doctors and nurses stared at her child like at a rare lab specimen. The rarity was the fact that this fetus had survived until near term and was actually born, when most who suffer severe abnormalities are miscarried during the first trimester.

Afterward the students were allowed to return to their dorm as if nothing unusual had happened. Angelika remembered that none of them went back to sleep. Some cried and most spent the rest of the night in the residence living room, sipping tea and comforting each other.

But they were young and resilient, life went on, exams were passed and soon it was time for the rest of their lives to unfold. Angelika had big plans:

"I'll never return to our little town. I want to see the world! With my new found skills and my nursing diploma, I will have no difficulties."

Always loving different languages, she explored the possibility of working in the Swiss Alps to resurrect her French. She had contacted several excellent hospitals and healing spas and was waiting for a response. During this waiting period, right after they had taken state- boards, a strange occurrence changed their lives.

In the past they studied infectious diseases old and new and Angelika was especially interested in all that she could find out about plague. She learned that it still existed in the far corners of the world but had been mostly eradicated in Europe and America. So it came as a total surprise, when the staff at the hospital was notified of a plague outbreak in a nearby town, the same university town they previously transferred their critical patients to. There was a call for doctors and nurses to volunteer for the care of those afflicted with plague.

An underground hospital for severe epidemic outbreaks had been built many years ago, but up to this point it had never been used. A call went out for volunteers to aid the infected in this facility. This meant that doctors, nurses and other personel caring for the victims would not be allowed to leave until all were considered non-infectious and the time of quarantine was exceeded.

Angelika happened to be on leave, visiting Granny and Bella, when the call came, asking her to volunteer. Her eyes were big and serious when she read the simple instructions to them. She explained:

"I know in my heart, that this is the right thing for me. I have studied plague extensively. Besides my experience goes back hundreds of years," she joked.

"You must not act foolish child; you had a dream, that's all, nothing but a dream," replied Bella while Granny looked positively frightened:

"You must be smart and not expose yourself to a deadly disease at your age. It would be such a waste if something happened to you!"

"Granny, I have been around disease, death and dying just about all of my life. I am healthy as a horse and I shall have to go. Don't you see; it was a premonition. I am meant to go. If I don't, I will regret it for the rest of my life. I am convinced of that and that would be worse than death." Big tears gathered in Angelika's eyes, spilling down her cheeks during her last remark. At last they relented and Bella agreed:

"I suppose if you want to have a life worth living, you must go!" She jumped up and wiping her eyes with her apron, she made herself busy gathering different herbs and leaves and seeds from various jars.

"Here is what you take with you; it's all measured out. A few pinches in boiling water taken as tea every night without fail, will keep you well my dearest girl." She packed it into a large tin. "Promise you will not forget!"

"I promise, I swear."

Chapter 13

Healing Body and Soul in Real Time

The following morning Angelika, full of good wishes from her grand-parents and friends left on the early train to report as a volunteer at her hospital. It was early summer; a rainy day, thick clouds of mist were hanging low in the trees, shimmering like finely spun silk among the rain drops. Since it was packed to capacity Angelika had swung her suitcase with some difficulty onto the upper baggage rack. She did not know how long she would be gone this time. 'Probably more than three days', she mused.

Three years had passed since her dream and yet she remembered every single detail of her three day adventure that Bella had called a "day-scare" to the fullest. Even certain smells and sounds would break through occasionally reminding her of people and places she met there in that age of darkness. She always thought of it as a place of darkness, externally only lit by candles and oil and internally deprived of the enlightenment of new discoveries. She felt a bit drowsy, because she did not sleep much the night before, out of sheer excitement about the upcoming adventure. This time she was sure it would be an adventure in real time. She was just drifting off, leaning her head against the cold window pane, when she caught her reflection in the dark glass. A finely chiseled face with high cheekbones and big light brown eyes were assessing the world calmly under too heavy eyebrows. Pale cheeks tapered down to a small mouth decorated with a thin upper, but a generous lower lip. Dark brown wavy hair was tamed into a severe ponytail adding the finishing touch of the portrait. She was beautiful but did not think so nor did she appreciate her singular look, which did not agree with the public's idea of beauty. Those images coined by television and magazines showed tall women with blue eyes and blond manes on the verge of starvation with a silly disposition. She thought of herself as being of sound mind and average looks.

Soon enough the train pulled into the station, everyone got off and Angelika was in the process of lugging her heavy case the two mile hike to the hospital campus. When she arrived many others had gathered in the large employee dining room. An announcement was made for everyone to line up as quickly as possible for a physical which would determine whether one was fit in body and mind to volunteer for this cause. They had been told that the patient load up to this point had been fifty patients who had come down with a relatively new form of the plague. Angelika got in line with ten other nurses; three of them she recognized from her work in the hospital, the other seven were strangers. They were ushered into a large office and given a questionnaire, which asked about previous experiences with infected patients, a short family history including many medical questions such as height, weight, allergies, previous illnesses and surgeries. Angelika thought it all pretty straight forward. She had had all childhood diseases, but at the age of twenty-one she felt wonderfully strong and healthy. However when it came to her turn to be examined for blood pressure, pulse, and lung and abdominal sounds, she suddenly felt nervous.

'I wonder if I'll pass. If they find anything wrong with me I won't be allowed to go.' It was her greatest fear, for she knew in her heart that this call was meant for her. Illogically as it seemed, she was convinced that this most ancient of all diseases reoccurred just to prove her dream. She knew how irrational her thought process was, but could never shake the feeling of premonition.

The old doctor looked over his glasses with tired eyes at this young fresh faced greenhorn of a nurse, who was smiling to hide her insecurities. He most reluctantly signed the petition as 'able'. He did not want to send anyone to their possible demise and especially not the young ones.

"Have nothing better to do with your life?" he growled under his breath. "Did not get over a lost love, left at the altar or what the devil other reason would a young beautiful girl like you want to sign up for this hellish duty? Do you think being fresh out of school has made you invincible? If you think that, it has made you stupid!" He looked very grouchy and also very sad when he handed her the signed affidavit.

"No sir, I have not been jilted or disappointed in any way, I just......"

"Oh spare me the drama of wanting to save the world! Well you are healthy and strong, don't be foolish, you only live once!" With that he waved her away and started to insult the next person in line.

"Well that old coot better behave himself with me!" said an older nurse who had overhead the entire exchange with Angelika.

"You won't have any trouble; he does not mind about the old ones, it's the young he wants to talk out of being a hero," said a heavy-set woman across the aisle.

"Rightly so," cried a third. "We have lived our lives, they are only starting out. Let's see if we pass the physical first."

Angelika held on to her paper and moved along to receive further instructions. From the ten nurses lined up before the physical only six made it through. She felt lucky to be among them. Besides the nurses there were many other professions requested, such as lab and x-ray technicians and several young doctors as well.

"We would like to have a staff of sixty for right now," said an older gentleman, who seemed to be in charge of the selection program.

"Please take your completed paperwork and your luggage and follow me. The busses are lining up in the parking lot to take you to your destination. Now remember, you have been chosen to volunteer, but this is not your ordinary volunteer program. Once the sick arrive there is no going back. You will have a short orientation; see a documentary explaining the layout and your role, and then you will be taken on a tour. Besides the regular hospital wards, operating theaters, x-ray and other laboratories, we have a small movie theater, a grocery store, a small restaurant and bar and a gym with a swimming pool for our daily exercise."

He picked up his clipboard and started to read names. Once Angelika heard her name she moved up to the front. Soon all the busses were filled and they were off.

The entire process had taken the better part of the day. It was late afternoon and she had had nothing to eat since her breakfast with Granny. As she rummaged through her carry-on bag, she found next to Bella's tin a nicely wrapped package containing two meat sandwiches and a big hunk of Granny's pound-cake. Her hands were shaky as she unwrapped the first sandwich and took a big bite. She had been too nervous and had kept to herself and just now noticed the young woman sitting across from her who stared longingly at her precious sandwich. The seat right next to her had stayed empty.

"Would you like some? I have another and I think I can only eat one."

"I would love it," answered the girl in a high voice. "I have been too nervous to feel hungry until now." She got up and slid into the seat next to Angelika, who handed her the bread and a napkin.

"Good ol' Granny, if it were up to me we would be starving right now."

The girl bit into the sandwich with gusto.

"Hmm, ham and cheese, my favorite. We are supposed to get dinner tonight, after the presentation and after we have made our final decision. Do you think you are going to do it?" She asked with her mouth full.

"I have to," was Angelika's short reply. If the girl seemed surprised by that; she did not show it but continued chewing contently. When they were done with the bread, Angelika broke the pound-cake in half.

"Here," she offered, "Granny makes the best. 'Heart attack on a plate', as Grandpa calls it; eggs, butter, sugar, vanilla and a little flour to hold it all together."

The girl closed her eyes after the first bite grabbing her heart; she pretended to have chest pain. "Oh my God, it's worth it," she moaned. "Well let's see, if we survive Granny's cake, we'll probably beat the plague." They both started to laugh and Angelika finally got a good look at the young girl sitting next to her. She had a fine build and sparkly green eyes surrounded by a mop of bright red curls. Her mouth was wide and her lips so generous that she looked quite lovely. It was those small very white, wide spaced teeth that led you to think that their sharpness may match that of her mind, but only when she laughed. Angelika was struck by the difference a laugh could make. They had eaten away some of their nervousness and apprehension, when she struck out her hand, brushing off some crumbs with a napkin.

"By the way I am Angelika, nice to meet you!"

The girl laughed again, sharp little white teeth blinking like diamonds in the dim light of the bus, giving her again that feeling of apprehension.

"I'm Roseanne," she smiled. "You can call me...."

"Rose," Angelika completed the sentence for her.

"Have we met?" Roseanne smiled again.

"No, you just remind me of someone I used to know."

Their hands touched and Angelika felt warmth spreading all the way up her forearm.

"May I call you Roseanne?" she asked. "It's a beautiful name and it suits you." She thought, 'I could not possibly call her Rose.'

She closed her eyes and tried to remember the Rose she knew. There were really few similarities, a small build and red hair. But that smile; if eyes are the window of the soul, those sharp little white teeth made her green eyes somehow shark-like, lifeless, eyes without pity and remorse. 'Just let it go!' She forced herself to relax and stay focused.

With full stomachs the swaying of the bus made them suddenly sleepy, and they closed their eyes for a short nap.

Before long the bus stopped with a jerk. Angelika awoke with a start, her purse slid on the floor in front of her and she heard Roseanne say:

"This must be it, I think we have arrived!"

Angelika strained her eyes trying to look out of the grimy window.

"I can't see anything," she mumbled. "Not even a building."

"It is supposed to be underground," said Rose. "No wonder the bus stopped suddenly. I am sure that the driver could not see anything either."

It was dusk; that short time of the day suspended between light and dark, loved or hated. Dawn was Angelika's favorite time of the day, the time when all possibilities still lay open, but dusk always meant to her a special time of reflection upon what had passed as well as the preparations for the wonders of the evening and the night. Dusk, the gateway to all kinds of thought provoking ideas and pleasures; a spectacular sunset, the reward of a day well lived or the comfort for a day well suffered. It did not matter. The light is always different; even without a sunset, its glare shielded by clouds, the light filtered by fog and dust gives the feeling of extraterrestrial splendor never observed at day time.

It was almost completely dark when they arrived at their destination. They were reminded not to leave anything behind as they stepped out into the dark. This group of about thirty volunteers found themselves under a glass shelter. The leader lifted his arm, and pointing to the left hollered:

"Follow me and mind your steps! We are going through a stand of trees and shrubs here."

When they got closer Angelika noticed a gate almost completely hidden by pine trees. It opened automatically and allowed the group to march through.

It was a relatively slow progression since everyone was weighed down by their suitcase and one bag which was the allotted amount of luggage they were allowed to bring. At the end of the path the sign 'Underground Facility For Infectious Diseases' pointed the way to an elevator on the right and two escalators on the left. Roseanne and Angelika took the escalator down about three stories much like the descent to a subway station. Another sign pointed them in the direction of the reception hall. Inside several other groups were already seated and sipping refreshments. The girls found two empty seats and gratefully put down their cases. Angelika declined alcohol because she wanted to keep a clear head while making her decision; whether she was going to stay or leave after the presentation. They were told that the busses remained upstairs until morning. They were also told that in spite one's good intentions, it might be impossible for a claustrophobic person to work underground, knowing that he or she would not be able to leave for a set amount of time, regardless how spacious the area might be. Angelika sipped water and Roseanne cheered herself up with a glass of cool white wine while they watched the presentation.

The hospital was a solid underground bunker. There was the house of beds for the patients on one side with laboratories, operating rooms and the pharmacy located in the right wing of the structure.

On the other side were the quarters for the volunteers, the kitchen, a general store, a movie theater and the recreational area with a small swimming pool and a gym. They were told that they were now gathered in the movie theater. The stage could be converted to a screen and all seats were movable and could be arranged to accommodate different events. The entire facility was brand new and had never been used but was designed for such an occurrence as this epidemic. They were also told that they expected some glitches to occur, even though all the emergency drills which had been implemented over the years had been successful. Angelika found the place fascinating although the idea of being captive underground for perhaps several months seemed daunting. Roseanne looked around with her bright green eyes and thought that since the pay was almost double of that on the outside, she could put up with just about anything for a time. Besides, she said that this hospital was lot nicer than the one she had worked in before. That one was old and dingy and no matter how much they scrubbed, it always smelled awful.

Angelika thought: 'Sounds familiar, but I was only there three days.' Out loud she said: "Well, let's give it a try."

Next they were reassured that in case of an illness, not related to the plague they would be treated and, after quarantine, be relieved of their commitment and released.

After the film and presentation out of the group of sixty gathered together in the theater, ten got up and asked to be taken back to the bus. The rest stayed and waited for further instructions. Divided into three groups they were taken on a physical tour of the hospital starting with their living quarters, so they could safely deposit their luggage.

Angelika and Roseanne walked together and when they were counted out by fours they both ended up in the same room. It was a lovely suite set up like a hotel with the difference that each two bed unit had its own bath and toilet. A hallway in the middle divided the room, ending in a sitting area with counter space sporting a tiny refrigerator, hot plate and a little pantry stocked with tea, coffee and condiments. Above the counter in the cupboard were four glasses, cups, bowls, plates and some cutlery. They were too busy looking at all this brand new splendor to notice the other two women who had drifted off to the other side of the room. Roseanne threw herself on the bed in the far corner and Angelika took the one by the door. There were no windows, but pictures of windows on both walls. Angelika's showed a lovely old frame with a view out onto a flowery meadow and some leafy trees. She thought to herself, 'I will know every flower and have counted every blade of grass and brush stroke by the time I leave here.'

Roseanne's window picture showed fall; colorful leaves on various trees, and a blue sky and sunflowers completed the scene.

"Guess what's on the other side?" she said.

"Spring and winter!" they burst out together.

"Well the decorator obviously lacked imagination, but it's better than plain walls." Angelika jumped up and checked out the bathroom.

"Hey, not so fast, there is a fake Picasso over the toilet, or is it a Matisse?"

Roseanne laughed, "I see an eye and a nose, and not exactly where I would place it. I'll say it's a Picasso!"

"And I say we will have plenty of time to figure it out," added Angelika and while she was still enamored with the lovely new bath and the shiny faucets, Roseanne stuck her head around the corner and cried, "Hello there, we are fall and summer, you must be winter and spring over there!"

A dark haired girl about their age came around the corner. "Hi, I am Maryanne, you can call me Mary, and this is Elizabeth, my new found friend here."

"I go by Liz, but my grandmother calls me..."

"Elsa?" interjected Angelika. She had just come from the bathroom and sat down on her bed with shaky knees.

"Yea, that's right! How do you know?"

"Oh, it was just a hunch, Elsa is sort of old-fashioned."

"That's right; it was my grandmother's name."

Angelika's head was spinning. She was trying to take this all in; when a bell rang and a loud voice over the intercom asked everyone to return to the auditorium to finish the tour. On the way back she was trying to convince herself that these girls looked nothing like the ones in her dream, that it was all purely a coincidence. There have to be a million Marys, Roseannes and Elizabeths around.

"You are a thousand miles away!" Roseanne had watched Angelika's expression and noticed her growing apprehension.

"Are you going to chicken out?"

"Nope, I have to see this through, there is no other choice."

The hospital was, as expected, a state-of-the-art place of healing. Angelika was impressed by the many innovations making the art of nursing more effective and pleasurable to both the patient and the caregiver. Everything was automated. They were especially impressed with the automatic bedpan-washer. A soiled bedpan was placed into the holder of the machine. Once the door was shut, one had only to push three buttons, one for clean, two for sterilize and three for dry. Within minutes the pan appeared clean, sterile and hot. All equipment was sterilized in each unit. Needles and syringes were only used once and all discarded material was also sterilized before it went into the garbage bins.

The patient rooms were spacious and modern. The eternal spring, summer, fall and winter motif was unfortunately repeated in each room and throughout the facility. At the end of each ward a well- equipped sitting room with TV sets for those patients, who were fortunate enough to walk about, made it pleasant. Angelika noticed that the individual patient rooms did not have television sets but piped- in music. The whole place vibrated with piped-in music which ranged from jazz to classical. Two large patient wards could comfortably accommodate thirty patients each. They were told that during a true epidemic outbreak the hospital could treat between three and four times as many casualties.

Finally they were ushered into the dining area. The tables were set and Angelika realized suddenly how terribly hungry she was. Grandma's sandwich had worn off hours ago and the aroma of sliced meat and cheese made her mouth water. They sat down at long tables and were told that this was a welcoming dinner that was being served and that starting tomorrow morning they will have to help themselves from the buffet. On the table stood pitchers of water and carafes of red and white wine. While they helped themselves to drinks, the kitchen staff brought out platters of cold sliced meats, cheeses and various breads with all the fixings. When they were are seated; the head of the hospital Mr. Baker, introduced himself, welcomed everyone and lifting a large goblet of blood-red wine, proposed a toast. Angelika could not wait to fill her glass and nodding to her comrades said:

"Cheers, and lets dig in, I am starved."

"Hear, hear," answered Liz.

After dinner the heads of medicine and surgery, as well as all supervising personal were introduced and everyone was asked to sign their contract. The stage was set. Patients were to arrive in the morning. They were urged to enjoy tonight, since there was plenty of wine and they should relax for this could be the last carefree day in the near future. After their contracts were collected, the group was divided into teams according to specialty and level of experience.

Angelika belonged to the red team. She refilled her wine glass and got up to search for other members with the red name tag. Maryanne was waving wildly from across the room.

"Come over here Angelika; meet some of your teammates!"

A small group had gathered, all sporting red tags.

"We are the surgical team. You must have had experience in the operating room."

"I did," said Angelika, "unfortunately I did not like it as well as working the floors. It was too mechanical for me! The patients were asleep and the staff too cliquey."

"That's what I liked best!" said Maryanne. "We were in our own world. The patients got fixed for better or for worse and transferred back to the real nurses to be pampered."

"That just sounds so cold!"

Angelika understood the adrenalin rush which comes from performing a life-saving procedure, but she truly enjoyed the care of the patients on the wards where their humanity with all its frailties becomes such a challenge for patients and nurses alike.

"Oh, you are a dreamer, girl," Maryanne could not get over that attitude and refilled her glass with gusto, "besides the cutest doctors are always the surgeons."

"That could be true, but they are often the dangerous ones, too vain and conceited to admit defeat, a character flaw if you ask me."

"I concede!" Maryanne laughed and pointed out her play on words. Angelika was surprised at Maryanne's exuberance and forthcoming attitude. For her part she preferred the medical man, the doctor who thought deeply before he made a diagnosis and foremost listened to his patients before acting. The surgeons, on the other hand, seldom listened, for they had perfected their craft much like a good mechanic. When all parts seemed to be aligned in their proper place, the offending culprit excised or restored, their job was done. Operation successful, patient alive, next!

Angelika knew that attitude well and had suffered it often enough, while giving needed explanations and comfort to those lucky recipients of surgical skills. She considered medical doctors, those whose first love did not include cutting and bleeding, true physicians. In her opinion they were the dedicated ones; constantly striving to heal the body by not forgetting mind and soul through listening, feeling and smelling. A wise doctor once told her that anyone could be taught to perform an operation, even a chimpanzee, if the procedure was repeated often enough, but only a true physician would know, when the procedure should be performed. She thought about all of this while shaking hands with the red team.

"We are the lucky ones," proclaimed Maryanne, "no boring hospital wards for us. We will triage the incoming patients appropriately up front, but then we should be on our own, unless our expertise is required elsewhere."

One of the young men, Angelika had not seen before grabbed another bottle of wine, filling everyone's glass to the brim, declared:

"Down the hatch comrades; let's eat, drink and be merry, for tomorrow we may be no more!"

Angelika had been surprised at the group's exuberance and had started to relax and go with moment, when that last so familiar phrase brought her back to reality; but which reality? The one she was living now, drinking wine in an underground bunker with the elite red team, or the memory of those three days, which still haunted her many nights and kept her wondering for the last three years. It was the very song James had paraphrased from Dante's Inferno:

"You are a thousand miles away little girl; come on, take a sip, this is our time. Who knows what will await us tomorrow?"

Angelika roused from her reverie, picked up her glass: "Well down the hatch then, by all means."

She looked at the happy celebrating group of young men and women and could not help but draw comparison between their joyful faces and those in her dream. Up to this point, Bella and Granny excluded, she had never confided in anyone about her experience.

Bella suspected time-travel but did not know enough about it. She knew there were many different ways of escaping reality, but the idea of mind and body leaving together had her puzzled as well. For Angelika's sake, she did not rule it out completely. Bella's wisdom and acceptance of the unknown and unseen forbade it.

Now Granny, however, was cut from a different cloth. She was a pious woman, refraining from witchcraft, sorcery and fortunetelling of any sort. She believed in clean living which meant 'early to bed and early to rise' and in complete trust in the Lord. Every other notion she considered foolish, if not blasphemous. Even her acceptance of Angelika's gift was nothing more than good horse-sense combined with a dose of the divine; nothing special since she herself had lived with its wonder and carried the responsibility it brought.

Bella, who did not have the same intuition, was not a religious person. She claimed nature and its forces, good or evil, as her guide-post. She wrought from nature her gift of healing through the many herbs, potions, roots and mushrooms that she gathered and prepared. She never prayed, but meditated, only she did not call it meditation, a word she was not familiar with. She would close her eyes, rocking back and forth in her ancient rocker and say, "Let's have a good think!"

While Angelika had confessed most of her dream to Bella during times of 'a good think', she never elaborated on any of the details concerning her close friendship with Doctor James. No matter how hard she tried, the words never came. This mixture of confusion and shame forbade any further discussion not even with friends her own age, who often thought her weird; when she did not seem interested in dating seriously as they did. She would go to dances and had a good time, but usually broke off any budding relationships with eligible young men her age. She tried to fit in, but she could not shake the memory of James. She still had the jeans and shirt she wore during her three day journey into the 17th century. Even after many washings she could still sense that aroma, that certain scent, that mixture of carbolic acid and perhaps something ancient and beckoning.

"Enough of your day-dreaming, earth to Angelika!" A pleasant voice roused her from her musing: "Let's go to the auditorium and find out what kind of music and movies they have!"

Angelika looked into smiling brown eyes and took the offered hand while holding on to her wineglass with the other.

"Ok, let's go!" She emptied the glass with one gulp and joined the small group with red name tags in search of entertainment.

"Wow, Angelika, I am a little dizzy from all that wine," Maryanne admitted. "But I think this will be a great adventure, don't you agree?"

She was pulled along and soon spotted amidst her group Roseanne who was the recipient of a blue tag.

"We are ward sisters," she cried. "Oh well, I don't care, we were told we can always switch duties."

In the auditorium someone had started to play the juke box, which was filled with all kinds of different music, rock and roll, jazz and classical choices.

"Come on, let's dance!"

'Brown Eyes' grabbed Maryanne and twisted her around in a crazy jig.

"Puh, I am really dizzy now!"

Maryanne let herself flop heavily into one of the chairs.

"How much wine did you drink?" asked Angelika who had had a couple of glasses but did not feel any effect at all.

"Oh, I don't know," said Maryanne pointing at the young doctor. "He, 'Brown Eyes' over there kept filling it up."

"We'll let me take you back. I am beat, it's been quite a day and we have to get up early. They want us here at seven sharp." And with that Angelika took Maryanne's arm and dragging her along the hallway, tried to find the way back to the dorm.

Maryanne was wobbly on her feet, giggling the whole time, making Angelika wish that she had more wine herself, since Maryanne seemed to be the only one having fun. Roseanne was there; she had already unpacked and was sitting on her bed, furiously writing into her diary. Liz was asleep on the other side of the room. Roseanne crossed her lips with her finger, trying to quiet them down:

"Sh, sh, Liz is sleeping, don't wake her up. She had a hard time; I think she regretted her decision to stay."

Maryanne wobbled over to her bed, flopped down on top of the covers, turned on her side and was out in a minute.

"One would think, that she could tolerate more with her size," said Roseanne coldly.

"Liz can still return tomorrow morning before patients arrive, if she still feels like that, but how about you?" Angelika asked.

"Oh me, I am here for the duration." Roseanne shrugged her shoulders. "I don't really know why, I just had a feeling like I was meant to volunteer." Roseanne's little white shark teeth blinked in the dim room, again giving Angelika that feeling of unease.

Trying to forget her dream and those comparisons, she quickly did her nightly ablutions in the beautifully gleaming new bathroom, enjoying the lovely hot water spraying from shiny faucets over her tense body in the shower. She had covered her hair because she did not want to lay down with wet hair nor make noise with the hair dryer provided for them. After brushing her teeth and creaming her face Angelika looked closely into the finely beveled mirror. She searched in the bright light but could not find that old-fashioned nurse from 1679. It was just Angelika, blinking back at her, no one else. So reassured she slipped her nightgown and robe on and went out to get her book ready for bed, when she heard Roseanne call quietly from the kitchenette

"How about a cup of tea?" and with her red curls bobbing she held out a mug with steaming herbal tea.

Angelika paused and then started to laugh hysterically, no matter how hard she tried to suppress the laugh attack, the worse it got, until she ended up with streaming eyes and hiccups.

"No thank you," she finally managed.

"Have you gone completely crazy? Whats so funny about a cup of tea?" Roseanne asked, looking incredulous and seriously questioning Angelika's sanity.

"Perhaps I will explain it to you some time." She was still smiling when she tucked herself into her blankets and left Roseanne wondering.

It must have been good wine, for they all slept soundly and dreamlessly until a gentle alarm over the intercom roused them with happy music and instructions for the morning.

They had been issued scrubs and white lab-coats the day before, so dressing was without options and fast. The girls jumped quickly into their clothes and did a short wash before gathering in the dining area. Liz, who was also assigned to the blue team, took Roseanne's hand and thanking her for the pep talk the night before told them that she had decided to return on the bus right after breakfast, if it was possible.

Breakfast was subdued even though the buffet looked wonderful, laden with sweet rolls, doughnuts, cereals as well as pans of scrambled eggs and bacon. But Angelika was not hungry and only took a sweet roll and coffee. Maryanne, who looked quite pale, avoided all food, greedily poured more coffee in order to swallow two aspirin tablets.

"I guess all that good wine was too much of a good thing last night," she mumbled. "The food is making me nauseous."

Liz seemed to be the only one with a good appetite.

"I know that I have made the right decision," she declared. She hugged the remaining three and went back to her room to pack. She was not the only one who had second thoughts. A small group had gathered outside the dining room and was now escorted back to the waiting busses for departure.

"It was just too confining for her here," explained Roseanne. "She was raised on the farm her people had for generations, you know. Wide open spaces, meadows and fields covered only by big sky not concrete boulders."

"I know," said Angelika, thinking about her Elsa, the sturdy farm girl, so good hearted and so capable.

"And how do you know?" Maryanne gave her a surprised look, but was almost immediately distracted by "old Brown Eyes" from last night, who looked just as bleary as she.

The group of initial volunteers had dwindled to about twenty-five. Soon the different teams took their positions in their assigned units and the fun was about to begin.

Maryanne and Angelika occupied their place at the frontline of the admission area when the first casualties arrived. According to the severity of their symptoms, patients were categorized and then placed into the perspective wards. All had been diagnosed previously and had received their initial antibiotics. Most were feverish but lucid and all had swollen glands. Two young men of African descent appeared more compromised than the rest and were admitted to the intensive care unit which was located right next to the operating suite. The set-up was interesting and completely different to what Angelika had experienced before. All the nurses and the doctors wore scrubs, masks, gowns and protective shoe coverings. Once you entered the OR and ICU suites, one could not leave without going through a disinfection chamber. One had to discard all clothing and step into a shower before entering the clean dressing area. The chamber and dressing area were different for men and women. 'Thank God!' thought Angelika.

Once she entered the ICU, Angelika was certain that she would be there for the next twelve hours until she would be relieved. Compared to what she was used to, this was easy work. Towards the end of her shift, they had admitted six patients; none of them in life threatening condition. Always alert to the needs of her patients, Angelika consistently noticed a steady pulse and a strong life force within everyone she had treated. Maryanne was grossed out by their swollen glands in groins and under arms, but Angelika thought that it was nothing compared to what she had experienced before.

They were informed that plague, the most ancient of all contagious diseases, which had killed one half of Europe's population in medieval times, was now well controlled and cured with antibiotics, but it remained extremely contagious, the bacterial culprit nearly unchanged from its original make-up.

In spite of the relative ease of the work, they were only too glad when their shift was over, when relief came and they could rid themselves of scrubs, masks, gowns and gloves, step through the shower and be free for the next twelve hours.

Once back in their room, it was time for another shower to wash off the disinfectant. They were only too glad to get back into their jeans and T-shirts and feel normal again.

"I wonder if we will have any skin left, when we get out of here." Angelika stared at her wrinkled hands and feet.

Once they felt presentable, they walked over to the staff dining room to check out the menu for the evening meal. The buffet looked scrumptious; roast beef, gravy, mashed potatoes, green beans and chocolate pudding with whipped cream. There was also a refrigerated section with yoghurt, fruit and sandwiches for the small appetite or for those who missed the dinner hour. They stood in line and agreed to have the beef. Maryanne decided to stay away from all alcoholic beverages, but Roseanne and Angelika reached almost greedily for the red wine. Old Brown Eyes, the young and friendly doctor from the night before joined them and explained that the wine was indeed superb; one of the best Burgundies he had ever tasted. Angelika was no judge of quality wines, since she never had the funds to develop a taste. As long as it did not pucker her cheeks or burn her throat on the way down, it was acceptable in her opinion. Maryanne did not remember its quality only its potency and was afraid of its effect on her judgment, but Roseanne's eyes lit up, she had no such qualms and refilled her glass already for the second time. Angelika sipped slowly and noticed, since she was seated directly across from Roseanne, that her snow-white little shark teeth had taking on a bluish red stain. Her expression appeared unchanged when serious, but during her loud and unrestrained belly laughs the exposed wine-stained sharpness of her teeth gave her a vampire likeness, as if she had just sated herself with the blood of her victim.

'I need to stop making up these stories and comparisons,' Angelika forced her mind and her imagination to focus and foremost to forget.

"And what has made you so thoughtful?" The young doctor focused his attention on her.

"Oh nothing, I am just tired I think, and the wine is not helping."

"No wonder, all this is new and unfamiliar. Once we know where everything is located and catch on to the routine, it will be easier," he said. More people joined them at their table and the conversation thankfully turned to the management of the patients and how to establish a functioning environment of healing.

It was getting late and Maryanne who had stayed stone sober, reminded everyone that tomorrow was another day and that they should all get a good night's rest.

"Oh, speak for yourself, what happened to the party girl from yesterday?" a young fellow from the x-ray department joked.

"She may be a party girl, but she is also a fast learner!" Maryanne laughed. "I underestimated the effect of this good wine."

"Well, what do they drink where you come from, tea and milk?"

Maryanne was ashamed to admit that he had hit the nail on the head. As forward and brusque as she could be any given time, she never quite got used to alcohol.

"We don't have to make a fool of ourselves every day," Angelika was trying to defend the girl, who was obviously uncomfortable with this line of questioning.

"Oh, what the hell, we did not drink wine at all, perhaps some ale or beer on Sundays with our meal. So there you have it, my working class background. I am not of your pampered lot."

Angelika heard 'beer and ale', saw the contrite face of Maryanne and the gleaming one of Roseanne, and decided then and there that this was a good time to end that gathering.

"Let's go Maryanne! You are absolutely right, I am also tired and we need to function tomorrow morning."

"You are such party poopers!" Roseanne cried. Then she took the doctor's hand and pulled him to his feet. As if the man had his own reservations about Roseanne, he stood up slowly, turning helplessly back towards Maryanne and Angelika, before being dragged along by a raucous Roseanne.

The wine had made Angelika feel sleepy and she was glad to return to the dorm room. After they got ready for bed, Maryanne asked her if she would like a cup of tea, which she accepted gratefully. Thinking about the tin with Bella's herb-mixture she would add, she replied:

"I would like that. There was too much food and drink to lie down. A cup of hot tea will aid digestion."

The room had gotten chilly so they climbed in together under Angelika's blanket and warmed their hands on the hot mugs. After some moments of silence Maryanne asked:

"Now you must tell me what it's all about! I noticed how you looked at Roseanne with apprehension and you just about choked on your wine when I mentioned ale and beer. Besides, I cannot shake the feeling that we have met before. How is it possible, this feeling, no, this realization of a déjà vu so powerful, that it is undeniable? Yesterday I thought it was just the excitement of the first day, then the wine, but today I refrained from drinking, because I wanted to be clear-headed and not be fooled by alcohol induced speculations."

She put down her mug and took Angelika's hand. "Tell me, have we met? You are not from my town, but do you know my family? I know we have a connection, I am convinced of it."

Angelika continued to hold Maryanne's hand and started to speak quietly:

"If I tell you what has been haunting me and has not let me rest for the last three years, you must promise to keep this a secret and not doubt my sanity for I have doubted it myself."

While still holding Maryanne's hand, she felt her strong life-force combined with her good will and was finally moved to tell the story of her dream starting with the drowning death of her school friend. Maryanne's eyes were large and compassionate. Their tea grew cold and untouched in their mugs, when the tale unfolded.

Angelika left nothing out, well almost nothing and when she came to the end; her end, describing Mary's recovery, Maryanne's eyes spilled over with tears and she started to sob.

"I knew it!" she cried triumphantly, "This connection, even though I don't understand it. I felt it the first time I laid eyes on you. Now let me get it straight. Roseanne may well be your Rose. We agree, she has an evil streak and Liz was your Elsa. It all fits! Doesn't make a bit of sense, but it fits."

Angelika was shaking her head. "There is but one missing, Dora, sweet Dora, who loved Mary deeply."

At the mentioning of Dora, Maryanne buried her head in her hands and started to rock back and forth.

"Oh my God, How could I forget? Dora is not missing."

"She is not?" Angelika looked confused, but Maryanne continued:

"This is crazier than I thought. Your Dora was my Doreen, a neighbor girl. We grew up together. Oh God, Angelika, when we were very young, only in junior high, she admitted to love me. Can you believe that? We were so young and I laughed it off and told her that she was crazy and if she was not crazy, she was perverted. I never spoke to her again and she avoided me from that moment on. The following year she and her family moved away. I never heard from her again."

Angelika was stunned speechless, but Maryanne was not to be stopped:

"You said this dream happened to you three years ago."

"That's right, three years ago almost to the day."

"Three years ago I was already nursing when I contracted pneumonia from a patient. I was very ill for some time and suffered a high fever. Some days I was delirious but I don't remember dreaming."

Maryanne looked quite shaken.

"It's all a mystery to me," Angelika admitted. "I feel sorry that I have upset you so. It was not my intention. However, I must say that I feel better, lighter somehow now that you know. In time we might figure it all out and get some better understanding."

"But there is something else that bothers me." Maryanne was now adamant to get to the bottom of this story that somehow involved her. She was like a bulldog, not letting go.

"I noticed how you handle your patients. It is not only with reverence, but also with expectancy and caution in the same way someone would pet a strange dog. There is hesitancy, as if one is not sure of its demeanor."

Angelika laughed at that. "Well nobody ever put it quite like that, but you are very astute." She then elaborated about the fact that she was able to detect a person's life-force through touch and that she had this gift or curse for as long as she could remember.

"I knew it!" Maryanne cried triumphantly. "I knew you were some kind of a witch!"

"A good witch, don't worry! You and all our friends will live for a long time, at least until tomorrow," Angelika laughed.

"Well, you have not lost your sense of humor." Maryanne gave her a bear hug: "Friends forever and now we are waiting for Mr. Right!"

"He is not here. I know that much!"

Angelika's smile vanished and Maryanne added with a serious face, "It's only been one day. Remember it took three in your dream."

Once they realized how late it had become, they decided to call it a night. Maryanne went to her side of the room and climbed under her covers. Neither girl fell asleep for a long time. Finally Angelika heard even breathing from the other side of the room mixed with gentle snoring. Even though she kept her eyes shut tight, she could not find rest. She heard Roseanne stumble into the room awkwardly, bumping into chairs in the dark and hitting the side of her bed before collapsing onto her covers and almost immediately starting to snore.

Morning came too soon for all of them. Angelika had lain awake for the longest time, listening to the even breathing and snoring of her roommates. Roseanne looked worse for the wear. Maryanne and Angelika exchanged conspiring glances. They got ready quietly. Roseanne displayed a severe sensitivity to noise and held her head when Angelika accidently dropped the tea mug into the sink.

"I think I have learned my lesson as well," she moaned, still clutching her pounding head.

"Perhaps that wine is not as great as we thought, or somebody overdid it!" Maryanne showed no sign of sympathy.

"Well, whatever it is, let's go to breakfast, I am starving!" Angelika could not believe that she was actually hungry again. This time she did not shirk the rich fare of eggs, bacon and pancakes. Maryanne followed suit, but Roseanne hung back and only stared at her steaming mug of coffee.

"I can always grab something later," she said. "You girls are much more confined than I."

The next twelve hours passed as in a daze and without any incident. Some patients were well enough to leave and were transferred to a regular ward. Others came and took their place. At the end of their shift the girls followed the same cleansing routine and gathered once again in the dining room.

Dinner was a quiet affair. Not even Roseanne, who seemed quite recovered at this time, poured any wine. They were tired and somewhat disenchanted. All were thinking of how in the world they would be able to maintain their strength and sanity in this confining world of sickness. No one felt like listening to music or watching a movie. Everybody retired early, hoping to escape through sleep. They were told that it was not unusual to feel somewhat depressed after the newness of the place and the euphoria of the first day passed. It was all a matter of adjustment and patience.

The following morning they started out rested and hopeful that during this third day of their mission the apprehension would lift and that they could return to their task renewed in body and spirit.

Later in the afternoon two relatively sick patients were admitted to the special care area. Unfortunately one young man from the Far East had not been diagnosed early enough. His symptoms had been vague and then exploded into the pulmonary type of the plague. He was having trouble breathing and was now fighting for his life on a ventilator in Angelika's care. They had bombarded him with multiple antibiotics but they did not seem to help. His lungs were filling up and he needed chest tubes to drain the fluid. At this time none of the volunteer doctors had the required training to insert the tubes and to perform the necessary surgery to create a permanent window in the thick covering of the patient's heart. Angelika feared for the life of this man. His pulse was weak and irregular and she knew without a doubt that his time on earth was limited without further intervention.

While it seemed hopeless, she was told that a heart specialist from a local hospital was ready to volunteer his time to perform the needed surgery.

Anxiously awaiting his arrival, the patient was prepped. All nurses and doctors were gowned, gloved with head and shoe coverings wearing facemasks and protective eyeglasses.

Dressed like this, Angelika met the young and brave doctor in order to assist him with the procedure. They mumbled a quick 'hello' and then Angelika took him to the struggling patient. She noticed how this tall physician bent down to examine the poor man and the gentle way in which he lifted his shirt and listened carefully to his chest. She helped him turn the patient on his side, when their hands touched.

As if struck by lightning they both let go and pulled back nearly dropping the patient. Stepping away from the bed, they pulled of their facemasks and eyeglasses and stared at each other.

"How do I know you?" he asked quietly. "We have not been introduced." Angelika took off the glove of her right hand and held it out to be grasped.

"Hi, I am Angelika."

"I am James Merlin."

"I know. I was waiting for you!" she whispered with a Mona Lisa smile.

Epilogue
What is Plague?

Plague is often referred to as 'The Black Death' (black boils called buboes developed on the body of the infected) coming from China and spreading its terror along the Silk-Road from the seaports of Italy and France throughout Europe during the 14ᵗʰ century. Evidence suggests that it was the first epidemic which infected humans.

Rain fell almost constantly during this century in Europe; rotting crops and therefore leading to starvation. An increase in the rodent population combined with the weakened condition of the people led to widespread disease and ultimately to plague. It is estimated that about one half of Europe's population got wiped out by plague within five years.

New research has proven that medieval plague is not much different from its modern cousin by examining 1200 corpses from plague victims buried in the East Smithfield Cemetery in London. Researchers looked at the inner chamber of teeth where a black powdery substance composed of dried blood and nerves was a goldmine for DNA excavators. Using the modern strain of the plague bacteria 'Yersinia pestis', named after the French bacteriologist Alexander Yersin, they were able to achieve a nearly complete reconstruction of the 'Black Death' strain. It is fascinating to know that unlike other ancient strains of bacteria, plague is almost identical to its medieval cousin.

There are 2000 cases of modern plague reported worldwide each year. Rats and fleas spread the disease just like it did in ancient times. Modern antibiotics treat plague effectively and, according to scientists, would have treated the medieval strain as well. Unfortunately for those living during the middle ages Tetracycline was not developed until 1952.

(From an article by Elizabeth Landau CNN health writer)